Crossing Charry Ridge

Praise for Crossing Charry Ridge

Just as Suzann Albright has given us characters we can genuinely care about, she has issued, in *Crossing Charry Ridge*, a compelling wake-up call and an invitation to connect with and perpetuate the rich and time-honored Southern Appalachian culture that is sadly on the threshold of being lost forever. -- **Rich Follett** for Readers' Favorite.

The storytelling and factual knowledge blend make this novel entertaining and educational, offering a unique reading experience. -- **Inhouse Book Critics**, Mainspring Books

In her incredible debut novel, Suzann Albright touches on many significant topics, like the protection of the environment, abusive behavior by a parent, or the death of a loved one ... This is a profound and almost philosophical book ...The book highlights the value of forgiveness and understanding, ending on a high note and giving us food for thought ... The cover illustration by the talented Pamela Murphy reflects an intense scene described in this fascinating tale. -- **Nino Lobiladze** for Readers' Favorite

Crossing Charry Ridge

A NOVEL

Suzann Albright

Blackest Crow Publishing

Second printing, with minor revisions

Print ISBN 979-8-9878807-2-2
E-book ISBN 979-8-9878807-3-9

Blackest Crow Publishing
P.O. Box 992
Floyd, Virginia 24091

Website: suzannalbright.com

The pencil drawing on the cover was created by Pamela Murphy.

First Printing, 2023

**For the southern Appalachian Mountains
and all who know that place as home**

"There are only two things
we can hope to give our children:
One is roots and the other is wings."
— Hodding Carter II

Contents

Web Extras

If topics in *Crossing Charry Ridge* spark your interest and you would like to learn more, you can visit the companion website for this book. There you will find general background information on the Blue Ridge Mountains and their inhabitants, including images, audio clips, and videos that complement the story.

SUZANNALBRIGHT.COM

1

Survival

Before All Else

When the mothers and fathers of all our fathers and mothers first landed here, they brought her a name from the Cherokee. Her sweet breath was the first we breathed, her rocking was the first we felt, and the first we heard was her singing in the Language of All Beings. Before we knew that we were blind and naked, we knew only her. We call her Owenasa—Home.

My brother and I were always hungry. Sometimes I was too weak to hold my head up. My brother was bigger, so he could cry louder for food. Sometimes he pushed me over and grabbed my portion. Still, I managed to get enough to stay healthy and grow stronger daily.

Often as he could find it, Paw brought food for Maw and us. Whenever Maw had to leave us, he stayed close by. Brother and I were quiet then. We huddled together and drowsed and waited. It was Maw who protected us and sheltered us from rains and bitter winds of mountain springtime.

Maw and Paw had built this place themselves of the sturdiest materials they could find. It was their first home together as a couple. Shortly after they finished construction we arrived—first brother, then me.

Our parents had come from big families, and had helped care for their younger siblings. So they had some idea of what would be required of them as parents. They did their best to provide for us, but life was hard. Sometimes relatives would stop by with gifts of extra food for us ravenous young ones.

After a while, I began to sense light. Gradually, my vision improved. Brother appeared first as a hazy pink lump. Maw and Paw were black as my blindness.

My hope now is to share my experiences as I grew from the modest beginning I have described into the being that I am now. I ask only that you let your imagination take flight, and envision our world through the eyes of a crow.

Attack!

Light and darkness followed light and darkness. Sounds began to matter more. Our vision became more acute. Fluffy gray down grew over our pink, bulbous bodies. Then spiny pin feathers poked out over our backs, wings and tails.

Gradually, black feathers emerged from those white spikes. We grew strong enough to move about in the nest. But we were not nearly prepared to fly or to search for food.

Always, one parent brought us a meal. The other parent, usually Maw, guarded us. One morning Paw left to search for food. We waited and waited, but he did not return. Then Maw left. We were alone.

We were hungry, but we knew better than to cry. Attracting attention could be dangerous. As we waited, fear outgrew hunger.

Brother spotted the threat before I did, and he alerted me. A red-tailed hawk was coming at us fast. Her sharp beak could tear us to shreds. Brother bravely rose as tall as he could, spread his wings, and flapped furiously.

I tried to position myself a little higher. My plan was to peck the hawk's eye. Brother and I could fend her off together, I was sure. I hopped up to the edge of the nest. But I was clumsy. I teetered. I lost my balance.

It seemed to me that I fell slowly. I struggled to right myself. My scrawny wings tried to catch the air. No use. I somersaulted to the ground and rolled on the blanket of leaf litter.

That was my first landing. Luckily I didn't break my neck, but I was still in a world of danger. All alone.

Capture

Our parents had taught us about predators. I knew they were not all birds, like hawks and owls. There were many predators that could attack on the ground as well as in the trees. Snakes, feral cats, bears, bobcats, even squirrels could be deadly for small crows. But the most dreaded threat—the creature all wild things fear—is a Person.

I shivered. I thought of my brother. I hoped that Maw or Paw had gotten home in time to save him. And I hoped that one of my parents would rescue me.

Perhaps a shrub would be safe place to hide until help arrived. For shelter I hopped to a poplar sapling. How would my parents find me if I stayed quiet? I cried out loud as I could.

I heard the sounds of crushing leaves and snapping twigs. I stopped crying and listened. I heard a terrifying sound, such as I had never heard. It was a weird, unnatural vibration. Instinctively, I knew it was the voice of a Person. I froze.

"Hey there. What's the matter? What are you doing out here all alone? You must be an orphan. Don't worry. I'll take care of you."

The Person was standing on his back feet, just as Maw and Paw had described. It had something black on its chest. It held that up to its eye and pointed it at me. The black thing made a quick snap, then a whirrr sound.

The Person crouched in front of me and slipped something off its back. It was another head. This head did not talk. The Person opened the mouth of the head. The mouth made a zzzzip sound. The Person pulled things out of the head.

Then the Person grabbed me. I struggled, but could not get out of its grasp. It drew me closer to the gaping mouth of that empty head. The Person was going to feed me to it! I screamed for Maw. No use.

It forced me into the head. Zzzzzip. The mouth closed and trapped me inside. It was dark in the head. I was all alone.

I felt the head being lifted up. It thumped against the Person's back. I joggled inside. The Person was moving, and I was rolling from side to side in the head. This, I thought, is what it's like to be eaten.

The Room

I could tell that the Person was moving more slowly and we weren't going down any more. Its feet made a different sound when it walked. We seemed to be going a little higher with every step. Up, up, up. We moved straight ahead, then it felt like we were turning around. The movement made me tumble against the side of the head. Something went click.

"Kevin, is that you?" a voice called.

"Yes, Mama."

The Person is called a Kevin, I thought. The voice is Mama. I didn't know where I was. It was too dark and too hot in this head. I was hungry. I wanted out. I started screaming for Maw.

"Kevin Wendell Ramsey! What on earth have you got in your backpack?" the Mama voice said.

"It's a crow, Mama," Kevin answered. So I understood that this thing I'm in is called a backpack.

"A crow? What in the world are you going to do with it?"

"I was fixin' to keep it for a school science project. I can take photos of it and train it to talk. Remember Uncle Dan said he had a pet crow when he was a boy, and it learned to say words?"

"Yes. Well… you are not keepin' it in this house. You can take it to your room, but just for tonight. Tomorrow, if you still want it, you can build a place for it out by the shed."

"Yes, Mama."

"And it can't stay in that backpack."

"No, Mama. I was wonderin' if Elaine would loan me her old puppy crate to keep it in for a little while."

"I'll call your sister and ask her. Now take it to your room and shut the door, so the cat won't get it."

"Yes, Mama."

"And wash your hands. Supper is almost ready."

"Yes, Mama."

"And you keep that bird quiet tonight. You don't have school, but your daddy has teachers' meetings all day tomorrow, and he needs his sleep. You hear me?"

"Yes, Mama."

I felt the Kevin moving forward again for a short distance. I felt that swirling around motion again, and heard another click.

"There. The door is closed, so you should be safe." With a zzzip sound, the jaws of the backpack came open. "Come on out now." The Kevin reached in, put his claws around me, and set me down on something like the ground; something very flat and soft, but smelly. I pooped on it.

I had figured out that I was in a place called Kevin's room inside a place called this house. The whole place reeked. It was full of smells I had never smelled.

It was horrifying to look at, too. Everything was a weird shape I had never seen. The sides of the whole space, the top and bottom of the space, and almost everything inside it had the same shape. Everything here had straight sides, and points. Wherever two sides met, there were points. The shapes made me feel edgy. It was sickening!

Then I saw a shape that had a piece of sky in it. It wasn't too high. If I flapped hard enough, maybe I could get into the sky, away from this awful room in a house. I jumped and flapped hard as I could. Bump! I hit my beak on the sky and fell down. That hurt. I puffed up my feathers.

"Whoa! No! You can't fly through the window. You OK? I'll pull down the window shade." Then I understood that that piece of sky is called window. Kevin reached up and pulled something that covered the piece of the sky. Shade is what makes a window disappear. "Here, sit on my bed. It's nice and soft."

Kevin picked me up and set me on the bed. It was soft. But it was the same weird shape as the window and everything else.

Kevin said, "You must be pretty hungry. I'll go see if Mama can find something to feed you." Kevin walked to one of the weird shapes on the side of the room and pulled it. One edge of it came open. He walked through the opening into another space.

Kevin looked back and said, "I won't be gone long. You behave." He pulled the shape back toward him, and it closed making that click sound I had heard before. I thought that shape must be the door Mama had mentioned. I was alone.

"Maw! Maw! Paw! Paw! Maw! Paw!" I screamed until I was exhausted. I closed my eyes and fell asleep.

A click startled me awake. Kevin was back in his room. "Sorry I was gone so long. Mama made me eat my supper first, but I got some food for you now."

He sat down. There were some wormy looking things on his feet, so I hopped over and grabbed them with my beak. Kevin pulled them away from me. "Hey now! You can't eat my shoelaces! Here, try this instead." He fed me something that made my hunger go away.

Kevin picked up a small item of that strange shape and pulled it apart, as if he were opening its jaws. I wondered if Kevin was going to feed it something too. "I gotta read a chapter in this book before I go to bed." Then I knew that thing was a book. Though the book wasn't doing anything, Kevin stared at it for a long while, but he didn't feed it. He shut the book's mouth and went out, closing the door behind him.

When he returned, Kevin had on different skin. He sat on the bed. "Good night, Jet," he said. "Stay quiet. I'll see you in the morning."

Kevin touched a shape on the wall and everything went black. I was blind again.

Morning

When I woke my vision had returned. I could see Kevin lying in his bed. He sat down beside me and said, "Hey, there, Jet!" He could see me! So this, I thought, must be morning.

Kevin put me into a different space. It was made of smooth, rigid sticks. Most of the sticks went up and down, but some went straight across. The top was made of the same kind of sticks. They made a ping noise when I pecked them. I could put my head between the sticks, but not my whole body.

This space was better than the backpack, because I could see and hear better. But it was the wrong shape for a nest. It was not cozy; it was crazy.

I did not want to be in this nest, so I hopped up and down. But my claws scratched on the hard flat bottom and made a racket. Kevin carried my new nest outside. Now I could feel the breeze on my feathers, see the sunlight, and hear other birds. Maybe Kevin would put me and my nest in a tree. But, no. He set it on the grass! Under a tree. Kevin doesn't know anything about nests!

I screamed at Kevin, until a terrifying thing came roaring up behind him and stopped. I pulled my head low between my wings and settled down on my feet to hide.

Call Me Jet

The roaring thing rolled instead of walking on legs the way Kevin does. Perhaps this was one of the "Persons Who Roll" that Maw and Paw had told us about. Those were especially dangerous.

The rolling Person's face was something like a Kevin's, but it had a beak. On top of its head was a large red spot, sort of like woodpeckers have. It stopped roaring and began talking like a Person. "Hey, Kevin! Whatcha doin'?" it said.

"Hey, Virgil! What are you doin'? You know you ain't supposed to ride an ATV on the road. You ain't even wearing a helmet. Where'd you get that?"

I guessed this loud thing is called a Virgil.

"Belongs to my cousin. He lets me ride it when he ain't usin' it. He ain't usin' it now, 'cause his leg's busted."

"How'd that happen?"

"This thing rolled over on him."

Kevin squinted at him. "How do you know it won't roll over on you? Does your Pap know you're ridin' that thing?"

"If he did, I wouldn't be ridin' it, would I?"

What the Virgil did next astounded me. It came apart! The part that was like a Kevin came off the part with rollers. Then it walked on its two back feet, the way a Kevin does!

After that, what the Virgil did was grotesque. It reached up with one of its claws, took hold of its beak, and pulled off the top of its head! Clean off! Or, that's what I thought it did, before I understood what baseball caps are. Actually, the top of its head was covered with hair as black as crow feathers. The Virgil turned around to the roller thing. It pulled out something green, and reached it toward Kevin. "Want a Mountain Dew?"

"Nope. Thanks. I'd rather keep my teeth."

"Ok," the Virgil said. It took the Mountain Dew, put it up to its mouth, and tipped its head back. "Ahhhh. Man, I was thirsty! You hungry? I got us a pizza at Pauley's gas station."

I concluded that the Virgil is a Person called "Virgil", instead of "Kevin". Persons have names.

"Pizza? Sure! Thanks! Let's sit over there at the picnic table."

Kevin and Virgil began tearing the pizza thing to pieces with their claws and biting it. Kevin shook his head slowly. "Gas station pizza ain't the best," he said with his mouth full.

"Nope. But it's pizza."

"Yeah!" Kevin said, licking his lips.

Looking at the big sticks stacked on the ground, Virgil asked, "So, what are ya buildin'? A chicken coop?"

"Unh-uh. A coop for my crow."

"Crow? You ain't got a crow."

"Right over there it is."

Kevin pointed at me with a piece of pizza.

Virgil twisted around and looked straight at me. His eyes and mouth opened wide as he walked toward me. I thought he was going to eat me and the pizza!

"Damn! Awesome, man! Where'd you git it?"

"Found it on Charry Ridge. It was cryin' and scared. I figure it's an orphan. I just put it in that puppy crate for now. My sister brought that over for me. Her dog's outgrown it."

"What are ya' gonna do with it?"

"I'm gonna take lots of pictures of it growin' up. I can write a report about it for school next fall. And I plan to train it to talk."

Virgil moved his head up and down. "Yeah. You take lots of pichures of ever thing. But teach him to talk? Good luck with that! How long you had him? Or her? What is it?"

"Found it yesterday. Uncle Dan says, you can't tell males from females til they're full grown. The males are the larger ones."

Virgil nodded his head toward me and asked, "You got a name for him—it?"

"I'm callin' it Jet."

"Jet. 'Cause it's jet black?"

I must be Jet, I figured. Crows can have names, too.

"Yeah. And fast like a jet. Crows are super fast. I read that they can fly 30 to 60 miles an hour. In a dive, they can go up to 70."

"Wow!"

"But Jet can't stay in that little puppy crate for long. It needs room to grow and stretch its wings. Besides, Mama won't let me keep it in the house no more. So I gotta finish this coop today. Lucky this is a non-instructional day. I got school tomorrow—and chores."

Virgil clapped his hands and stood up. "Alright, let's fall to it! I'll roll out that there chicken wire!" Virgil walked toward the stack of big sticks. "Got any wire cutters?"

Getting up and following him, Kevin said, "In the shed! Thanks, man!"

As the Persons worked together, they used tools that made horrible grinding and banging noises that hurt my ears. But I learned the words for all the tools they used.

After the Persons fastened chicken wire onto the big sticks

they called boards, they stood them straight up. Across the top they put something they called a roof.

From the shed Kevin brought things called latches and hinges to make a door on the coop. He carried the puppy crate into the coop, took me out, and set me on the grass.

This coop was huge. Kevin, Virgil, and I could fit together inside it. But the coop was of the same weird shape as the puppy crate. The same shape as the things in Kevin's room, and all the shapes on the outside of his house.

Kevin told Virgil, "I been feeding it cat food mixed with some oats and scrambled eggs. Wanna feed it some?"

Virgil fed me. It was just like gas station pizza—not the best. But I was real hungry, so I ate it all. At last, someone yelled from the house, "Kevin! Supper!"

On the ground outside were leftover pieces of the boards Kevin and Virgil had cut to build the coop. "Mind if I take some of them wood scraps?" Virgil asked.

"Help yourself."

"Thanks, Kevin." Virgil picked up some small chunks of wood. He got back on the ATV, and said, "See ya' at school tomorrow. Gotta jet!"

He waved his claw and roared away.

I knew one thing for sure. Kevin still had no idea how to build a nest.

Little Hero

Later, Kevin was walking from the house toward the coop with a strange Person. It said, "I want to see what you boys have built."

As they got closer, the strange one smiled and said, "Oh, you did a great job on this, Kevin!"

Kevin said, "Thanks! If it wasn't for Virgil helpin' me, I wouldn't have got the coop done today."

"I'm glad you boys finished, because I do not want that bird in our house. And you remember to wash your hands every time you handle it, you hear me, son?"

It held up Kevin's claw and gave it a shake. Then I understood that Persons call their claws hands and that Kevin and Virgil are called boys.

"Yes, Mama," he said. And then I knew that this strange Person was Kevin's mama. I had heard her voice before; but I had not seen her, and she had not seen me. They stopped just outside the coop. She bent over and peered in at me.

"Au-wuh!" she said in a high pitched voice. "It's a baaaa-bee! Son, you didn't tell me it was a baby. Its little eyes are still blue. Aww."

Her mouth blew a little breeze on me. "And it still has some of its down. You did the right thing, bringin' it home with ya, Kevin. Poor little ole thing surely would have died up there if you hadn't. I'm proud of you. You're a little hero."

She put her hand on Kevin's head and rubbed his short, reddish hair. Kevin moved his shoulders up. For a moment, his cheeks turned a bit pink, and the brown specks on his face seemed brighter.

Kevin's mama unlocked the coop door and came inside. She told Kevin, "Now, give me that food for it. I'll feed Jet. You run down in the cellar, and fetch that old dish pan. And bring me a big ole towel from the rag bag."

"Yes, ma'am!" Kevin ran back toward the house. He returned with a chipped white pan and a piece of blue cloth. He was breathing hard.

"Good," his mama said. "Now git your pocket knife and cut a big bunch of branches off that white pine over there."

Kevin came back with his arms full of branches. His mama placed them over the grass and up the sides of the coop.

She put the towel into the dish pan, and set me gently inside it. The pan was round, and the towel was soft. The green branches smelled like Owenasa.

Kevin's mama fed me the same sorry stuff Kevin and Virgil had given me before. But she talked to me in a sweet voice, stroked my head and neck, and told me not to be scared. I noticed something shiny on her hand. I pecked at it.

"Watch out it don't bite your finger, Mama!"

"Oh, it's OK. It's not biting my finger. It likes my wedding ring. Crows like shiny things."

"How did you know about taking care of a baby crow, Mama?" asked Kevin.

She smiled. "I was a Girl Scout. We are prepared. Listen. I'll look after Jet while you're at school. But when you're home, it's your responsibility, do you hear me?"

"Yes, ma'am. Can I take your picture with Jet?"

"How about I take one of you and Jet instead? Give me your camera." She held out her hand.

Kevin gave her the black thing he almost always had on his chest. He sat on the ground by me. Mama put the thing she called a camera by her eye and pointed it at us. It snapped and whirred.

Together, they left. I was alone. I knew one thing for sure. Kevin's mama does know something about making a nest!

Smokey

Kevin and his mama didn't come back. I walked about in the coop for a while, looking for a hole I might be able to fit through. No use.

I hopped into the fake nest Kevin's mama had made for me. I inhaled the light fragrance of the pine branches, pretending I was with Owenasa. The sky faded.

The evening medley switched from birdsongs to the chant of crickets and frogs. That music was a lullaby, and I began to feel drowsy. As I was on the very edge of slumber, I heard a scratching sound above my head.

I opened my eyes wide and stared. Something was moving through the high grass by the shed. Out from the grass a dim form emerged. The vague gray image silently inched toward the coop. It seemed to have a flat head, no neck, and no legs.

Slowly it came toward me. Closer and closer. Stopping. Creeping forward a little. I wondered what it wanted. I hoped it would whisper to me the secret of getting out of this horrible place.

Suddenly, four long legs seemed to shoot out of its body. It pounced, reaching toward the coop. Latching its claws onto the chicken wire, it began to climb. As it did, I heard a shriek.

A wide, black form dropped from the roof and grabbed the gray creature by its head. Letting go of the chicken wire, the gray thing fell backward onto the ground rolling and yowling. Its attacker released it.

A light flashed on outside Kevin's house. Mama's voice called, "Here, kitty, kitty. Kitty, kitty. Oh, there you are Smokey. What have you been up to, you naughty cat?" The light went out.

I hoped Mama had remembered to shut the door.

A familiar voice spoke. A voice I'd been desperate to hear.

The Fall

"I'm here, Little Darling." It was my own Maw's voice.

Maw! Where had she been all this time? Why had she abandoned brother and me? Why did she let Kevin kidnap me? I was glad to see her, but I had a lot of questions.

"Maw, I'm scared. Help! Get me out of here." She tried, but she was unable to find any opening or to undo the latch.

"Don't be afraid," she said soothingly. "I will watch over you, and bring you food. Someday you will be free. I'm sure of it."

"A boy called Kevin stole me from the woods. He's keeping me in here. He wants to take my pictures with a thing called a camera. He wants to teach me to talk."

"Talk!" Maw pulsed her wings excitedly. "Never do that! You must never say any of their words. If you do, Kevin will keep you forever. You will be a novelty to show off to his friends. Learn as many of his words as you can. But do not speak them! If you don't talk, Kevin may grow bored with you and turn you out. Please, heed my warning!"

"First, I want you to promise not to leave me again! Why did you and Paw abandon us? A hawk attacked us. We had to fight it all by ourselves. We were terrified. I'm sure brother told you what happened."

"Precious One, it is you who don't understand what happened. You don't know that your Paw and I never wanted to leave you alone for a moment. Let me explain.

"Your father went out early to scavenge for food along the road. He had never been gone so long before, and we were all terribly hungry. A raven witnessed what happened to your father. She took me aside, and told me the details.

"A Person in a roller threw out a paper bag with some food scraps in it. It fell in the center of the path where the rollers travel. Your father went after the food.

"He tried to snag a large piece of meat to carry home for us, but it was heavy. It slowed his takeoff. Another roller came up fast. It struck your father before he could fly out of the way. Raven said he was killed instantly.

"The news nearly broke my heart. But I knew I had to leave both my babies to find food for you.

"I was returning with a morsel, when I saw you and your brother fighting the hawk. You were both so brave! I saw you fall. The hawk flew off with your brother in her talons.

"I chased the hawk, but I was too late. When I caught up, she was perched on a limb, already picking flesh from your brother's bones."

"Oh, my dear Paw! Oh, my sweet brother!" I cried. "I fell out of the nest, because I'm puny and clumsy. That's why brother got killed. I should have been fighting by his side. I'm so sorry, Maw. It was all my fault. All my fault."

"You must not think that, Dear One! It's not true! You didn't fall because you're clumsy. You fell because brother pushed you out of harm's way. He pushed you back with his wing, so the hawk couldn't hurt you.

"Why do you think he often took more than his share of food? Because he always wanted to be big and strong enough to defend you, if need be. He felt it his duty as your older brother. That's why. He loved you, and would have done anything to protect you. I searched for you, and am thankful to have found you alive.

"Now, Precious Baby, you have only your Maw. And you are all I have left. I will do everything in my power to keep you safe. Believe me?"

"I do. And I promise you, Maw, I will never say a word."

Daily Lessons

Each day, Kevin and Virgil persisted in giving me speech lessons. Everyone in Kevin's family tried to get me to talk—including his sister Elaine and her little boy, Andy, who could barely talk himself. Kevin's Uncle Dan, who used to have a pet crow, gave it a try.

Some of Kevin's friends bet on who would be first to get me to say something. They all wanted to feed me, to have Kevin take their picture with me, and to offer words and phrases for me to practice. Their recommendations usually began, "Git him to say—."

I got lessons in how to say ridiculous things such as "pretty bird, hello, I'm Jet, shut up, smile, feed me, yoo-hoo, yum-yum-yum, play ball, you're so cute, and bye-bye." The most frequent words I heard were "hello" and "bye-bye" which everyone said to me on their arrival and departure.

I was an excellent student. To most of the Persons, I was a mere novelty in which they soon lost interest. They, however, were the intriguing subject of my concentrated study. I focused on their faces and memorized them. I studied their words, gestures, postures, and possessions. I memorized the names of every object they mentioned. After all, I had nothing else to do. And my survival depended upon knowing my captors and not letting them know me. Never did I say a word.

Without knowing it, Virgil was giving me counting lessons. When he came to visit, he usually had a Mountain Dew. He would flick the bottle caps into the coop for me to play with.

I amused him by picking up the caps and carrying them around in the coop. Whenever Virgil gave me a bottle cap, he would say something like, "Here ya' go. Now you have three toys." Or four, or five, or six toys. By the end of summer, I had ten. I practiced counting and sorting them in little groups, until I could add and subtract.

Meanwhile, I was also taking lessons the Persons never knew about. Maw was my teacher. She stayed nearby and brought me food every day. She gathered a variety of treats from dog dishes, garbage cans, grasses, stream banks, and the ground under bird feeders.

Sometimes, Maw dropped a morsel of food on the ground near the coop. Demonstrating for me, she held it down with her foot and pecked it repeatedly before pushing it through the wire for me to pick up. With the nourishment she provided and the stuff the Persons fed me, I grew quickly. I was no longer puny.

Maw described predators and warned me about those that might still try to kill me—snakes, rats, and owls especially. She said owls were particularly dangerous at night. They had the advantage of being able to see in the dark much better than we can.

Every night, Maw stayed on guard in a low branch of the tree by my coop. She never gave up hope that I might someday be free. But I had my doubts.

I knew quite a bit about Persons, but not much about other animals or how to live with them in the wild. Even if I could get free someday, would I really be able to make it out there?

The Party

Kevin was in the coop, tempting me with pieces of canned tuna, and asking me over and over to say, 'bye-bye.' Virgil strolled up. "Happy birthday, Kevin! Your daddy saw me runnin' here and gave me a ride," he said.

"Hey! Happy birthday to you, too, Virgil! Yeah, Daddy was out gettin' us some ice cream."

Virgil peeked in at me, and said, "Come on, now. Ain't you gonna say happy birthday to us, Jet? How's the speech lessons comin' along?"

"Not a word so far. Least not while I'm around."

Virgil chuckled. "Maybe it talks to itself while we ain't here."

Kevin stepped out of the coop and gave Virgil a little box with a bow on it.

Virgil handed something wrapped in brown paper to Kevin. "Thanks!" they said to each other at the same time. The boys opened their gifts right away.

"A Case knife! I can use this!"

Kevin said, "I know you like to whittle, so…"

Virgil fondled the knife handle and stroked the blade. "Yeah! This is great! Thanks, man."

Kevin's gift was a small statue. It looked just like a crow!

"Virgil, did you make this?"

"Yep. From a wood scrap you gave me after we built Jet's coop. My Pap ain't a Marine or a cop no more, but he's still particular about his shoes. He lets me use his shoe polish to stain my carvings."

"This is great! How'd you learn to whittle?"

"I learnt from Pap. It took a lot of practice." He splayed his fingers. "I got the scarred digits to prove it."

Kevin took a picture of Virgil with the wooden crow. "Come on. I want to take this inside and show my folks."

Soon, Kevin's daddy came across the yard carrying a plate of pink patties. He went to the grill and lit it, as I had seen him do many times. This family really liked to cook out. He laid some patties on the hot grill and they sizzled.

Kevin's daddy started giving me lessons. "Say 'bye-bye' and I'll cook a burger for you," he offered, pointing his spatula at me. But I knew from past experience that he would give me some hamburger anyway, so I said nothing.

The boys returned with a pitcher of sweet tea, some paper napkins and plates, and a stack of red plastic cups. Kevin's mama followed with a box of buns, bottles of ketchup and mustard, a jar of relish, and a big bag of chips. I liked chips, and was looking forward to getting some of those, too.

When the burgers were done, everyone sat on the picnic table benches, and mama filled each glass. Kevin's daddy said something about blessing. Every Person closed their eyes and held the hands of the Persons next to them. Then Kevin's daddy mumbled something, and everybody said Amen and opened their eyes.

Raising his cup Kevin's daddy said, "Here's to the birthday boys! Here's to friendship!" Kevin's mama said, "Happy birthday to y'all, and many happy returns."

When they had finished the burgers and chips, Kevin's parents went back to the house. Kevin's mama brought back a big brown cake. Kevin's daddy had a box of ice cream.

"I put both your names on here with icin'," Mama said. "See, this half is Kevin's and this half is for Virgil. And thirteen candles for each of you. I can hardly believe y'all are teens now."

She made fire on the candles. Kevin took a picture of the cake. Together, both boys blew out the flames. They all sang Happy Birthday to You. Whenever they sang the word "you" Kevin and Virgil pointed at each other. Everyone laughed about it. Mama cut a slice of cake for each Person.

"Nice!" said Virgil. "See, Kevin? I get more. I get half and you have to share your half."

Kevin's mama laughed. "Not so fast, Virgil. The rest of this cake is going home with you for your mama and your pap. So you will have to share your half, too. But you really will get more, because I happen to know your mama has a cake for you at home." She paused. "I wish they had come over. I invited them."

"Thank you, Mrs. Ramsey, we appreciate it, really. But they don't hardly go no place." Virgil took a bite of cake and licked icing from his lips. "Mmm. This is real tasty, ma'am."

"Here boys, have some ice cream with that," said Kevin's daddy, scooping out pink ice cream and dumping it on top of their cake.

Kevin's mama (now also known as 'Mrs. Ramsey') asked, "Do you boys remember when you first figured out that you have the same birthday?"

"Sure do!"

"Yes, ma'am!"

Kevin said, "Kindergarten. You and Virgil's mama both made treats for the whole class."

Virgil smiled. "Ever body got double cupcakes that day."

They all laughed again.

Kevin's parents gave each of the boys presents. To Virgil, they gave a fishing rod and reel. He was very pleased and said thanks many, many times. Kevin got a camera and binoculars.

When Kevin saw his gifts, he let out a whoop and leaped into the air. "My dream camera! Oh, thanks!" His smile stretched wide across his face. My, I thought, what big teeth Kevin has!

Kevin's daddy chuckled. "Son, you look about as happy as we were the day you were born." His mama smiled and nodded with her eyes closed.

After the meal was finished, Kevin and Virgil took turns feeding me tuna and scraps from the picnic. Everyone tried his best to get me to say, 'bye-bye.'

Kevin's daddy said it was about time for the news. He took Mrs. Ramsey's hand, and they walked back to the house. Bye-bye, I thought; but of course, I didn't say it.

As Virgil watched them walking away, the happy birthday look on his face faded. Virgil picked up a stick from the grass and started whittling on it with his new knife.

"You got kinda quiet. I hope all that wasn't too corny for you, Virgil. I mean, we've been doin' this same sort of thing every year for…"

"Oh, no! No way." Virgil shook his head. He stared at the ground and said, "You got a great daddy, Kevin."

"Yeah. Yeah, he's a good guy alright."

Virgil lowered his head and said, "I wish my daddy was a good guy…but he ain't. He's a mean, worthless coward, and he just got let out of jail again. Happy birthday to me."

Fever and Burn

"Your daddy was in jail again? What for this time?"

"Same as always—beatin' on people that can't fight back." Virgil tilted his head toward Kevin and pointed to a white line that split his left eyebrow. "You ever noticed this?"

Kevin nodded. "How'd you get it?"

"My daddy done that with a damned telephone receiver. He pounded on me like he was tenderizin' a steak. To this day, I won't put a phone up to that side of my head."

"Want to tell me about it?"

"Fever. It all started 'cause I had a fever. When I was little, Mama and Daddy and me was livin' in a run-down old shack way out on Curly Creek. You know where I mean?"

Kevin nodded. "I know 'bout where that is."

"We didn't have no neighbors close by, and it was a long walk to the road. Well, one day, when I was seven, I got sick at school and was runnin' a fever. So Mrs. Wilson drove me home."

"The one that's the school nurse?"

"Yeah. That one. My mama was fixin' dinner, but she stopped what she was doin' and started tendin' to me. She tucked me in bed, brought me some tea and all. You know.

"Daddy come home then, drunk as usual. He started yellin' at her that she was spoilin' me. He said I was gonna grow up a pussy because of her. He started poundin' on the table and askin' why wasn't his supper on it.

"Mama told him she was fixin' spaghetti when I come home sick. She had the water boilin' for the noodles. Supper would be ready soon.

"Well then, I got out of bed. Daddy shouted 'Soon ain't soon enough!' He went over and looked in the cookin' pot. He took aholt of the handle, and thew that bubblin' hot sauce at Mama's face.

"She put her arm up like this." Virgil raised his bent right arm, with the back of his his hand close to his face. He closed his eyes and turned his head to the left. "It splashed on her face by the side of her eye, and on her hand and arm she got burns. She's still got scars. That's why she's shy, and turns her face away, and won't look right straight at people."

Virgil spit on the ground. "So that's when Daddy punched her and knocked her out. He stepped on her hair so she couldn't git up, and kicked her in the side.

"I run to the telephone to call Pap. But Daddy seen me and yanked me by the hair of my head. He twisted that phone out of my hand and beat me with it."

Both boys were quiet for a moment.

"Virgil, I'm so sorry that happened to you and your mama. You know none of it was your fault, don't you?"

Virgil gritted his teeth and nodded.

"How'd you and your mama get away from him?"

Runnin' Scared

"Well, Daddy got thirsty again and started drinkin' 'til he passed out. I stayed awake. Mama... I could hear her cryin' all night.

"Luckily, the next day was a school day. Soon as it was barely light, I run out the door and thu the woods. Run hard as I could, scared that devil would wake up and chase after me.

"I hid behind a big ole tree by the side of the road. It wasn't til then that I noticed I was still wearin' my pajamas, and they was soakin' wet. I was the first stop on the bus route. Man, I never wanted to see a school bus so bad in my life. Finally, here it come down the hill and stopped.

"Mrs. Freeman was drivin'. When she opened them doors, I crawled up the steps on my hands and knees. Mrs. Freeman took a look at me and said, 'Lord Jesus in heaven, have mercy! Baby, what happened to you?' I told her my daddy hurt my mama real bad, and she needed help. I said I had to git back home and take care of her.

"I turned around, and them bus doors slammed shut before I could jump out. She said, 'No you don't, Baby. Your mama is gonna git help, but I'm takin' you to the doctor now.'

"So she got on the radio. She drove out to the intersection with 221, and met up with a police car. Next thing I knew, somebody was carryin' me into Dr. Muller's office. I was pretty out of it by then. Mama got taken to the hospital in the next county over. Some of her ribs was broke.

"Mama divorced Daddy right after that. Daddy went to jail, but he swore he'd git around to killin' us both someday. Mama don't feel safe, so we been livin' with Pap in his trailer. Pap says he seen a lot of this kind of thing when he was a cop. He says anybody that would harm a woman or a child ain't even a man.

"Mama don't go no place alone. She's scared of him findin' her somewhere. And I sorta worry that he'll come after one of us."

Kevin put his arm over Virgil's shoulders. "You were just a little kid. You did everything you could. You were real brave, Virgil. I know you've always been brave."

Virgil stared straight ahead. He wrinkled his brow and swallowed hard. "I swear, Kevin, if he ever touches my mama again, I'll…"

Virgil clenched his jaw. He stopped whittling on the stick, and threw his knife at a tree. The blade stuck in the trunk. "Well, I ain't sayin' what I'll do. But he's goin' some place he can't git out of."

Dr. Muller's Office

The next day, after Kevin had finished his morning chores, he came in and fed me. But for once, he didn't say a word or ask me to say one. He sat down on the picnic table bench and just stared. A while later, Mama came with a basket and said, "I saw you from the window, son. You hungry? I brought some sandwiches and cookies. Let's have dinner together out here."

"Um…yeah. Sure. Thanks, Mama."

Kevin's mama set out the plates and food and poured their drinks. Kevin bit into his sandwich and set it down. He stared at nothing in particular.

"Beautiful day, isn't it, Kevin?"

"Yes, Mama."

"Got any plans for this afternoon?"

"No, Mama."

"Son, are you feelin' alright?"

"Yes, Mama."

"Your daddy said that you boys were awful quiet on the ride over to Virgil's house last evening. And you were quiet and solemn at breakfast, too. Y'all didn't have a quarrel, did you?"

"Oh, no, Mama. Nothin' like that."

Kevin took a sip of his tea. "Mama, didn't you used to work for Dr. Muller a long time ago?"

"Yes. For a few years. I was the receptionist and office assistant for Dr. Muller. I worked to help out while your daddy was finishing his masters degree. At the time, Elaine was old enough to look after you for a little while until I got home. You remember that?"

"Yes, Mama. I'd forgotten about it, but now I remember."

"Why do you ask, son?"

Kevin drew a breath. "Well, I was wonderin' if you might have been there one morning when a little boy come in that had been hurt by his daddy?"

She set down her cup. "Yes. I remember when a little boy was brought into the office like that. Why?"

"Did you know who he was?"

"Yes, I did. Do you know who he was, Kevin?"

Kevin lowered his head. "It was Virgil, wasn't it?"

"Did Virgil tell you that last evenin' after the party?"

"He did." Kevin looked up at her. "Mama, why didn't you ever tell me? He's been my friend all this time and carryin' that around with him. I didn't even know."

"Well, I didn't tell you, because it was not my story to tell. If Virgil told you yesterday, it's because that was the right time for Virgil to share it with you. I guess he's big enough, and he trusts you enough to be able to talk about it now.

"Virgil does not know that I was in the office that morning. He was in shock when he was brought in. He was badly hurt. Dr. Muller examined him, treated him there, and went on to the hospital with him. I called the doctor's patients and cancelled all his appointments for that day.

"To respect the privacy of the family, the principal told other parents that the bus had some problems, and the other children on that route would be picked up late. The boys and girls in your class knew that Virgil had gone home sick the day before, so the teacher just let them think he was absent because he was still sick."

"I see. Mama, how could a father do something like that to his own family?"

She pursed her lips and shook her head slowly. "Virgil's daddy was a popular boy and a good athlete when he was young. But he drank a bit. Over the years it kept getting worse. He kept losing jobs, and he kept gettin' meaner. It happens like that with some people.

"I've known Virgil's mama since before you boys were born. Mandy Jenkins is a fine person. None finer. She put up with a lot until that happened.

"I will tell you something else, son. Mrs. Freeman saved Virgil that morning. And Virgil saved his mama. Your friend is a very brave boy."

"I know."

"I'm grateful y'all are good friends."

"Me too."

Daylight Star

Days grew longer, wetter, hotter. One scorching afternoon, the boys carried a cooler with ice and a watermelon in it out to the picnic table. Virgil put some of the ice into my water dish. That made it colder.

Kevin cut large slices of the melon. The boys made slurping sounds as they bit into the pink meat. Pink juice dripped from their chins and elbows.

They made a game of seeing who could spit the seeds farther. Virgil was a better spitter. I wanted to taste the seeds, but they didn't spit any to me.

Looking toward the sky, Kevin shaded his eyes with his hand and asked, "You think that one is comin' from Roanoke?"

Virgil looked up and squinted. "Prob'ly."

"Wonder where it's headed."

I cocked my head to see what they were looking at. High in the sky, a tiny light sparkled. A daytime star! A thin, white tail, stretched out behind as it moved across the cloudless blue.

"Man, I'd love to travel at jet speed. That would be so awesome," Virgil said.

"It is."

"You been in a jet before? When?"

"Yeah. Our family went by jet to visit my aunt Irene in Pittsburgh. She's a nurse at Children's Hospital. It was just a short trip."

So I realized that the daylight star was called a jet. It could travel in the sky like a bird. Very fast. That was amazing!

But the really incredible thing was that Kevin's whole family could make themselves small enough to fit inside a jet! They must have been as tiny as lice!

"That was a long time ago," Kevin went on. "I think I was about eight. I was pretty excited about the airport and watching the jets take off and land. It was a nice visit, too. Grandpa Ramsey was still livin' with Aunt Irene and her husband then. She took us to a lot of places in the city. We went to a Pirates game."

"Cool!"

"Yeah, but the best was when we went to the zoo. Aunt Irene bought me a disposable Kodak camera. She showed me how to use it, so I could take pictures of the animals."

"Yeah! Oh, I remember that now. When you come back to school, you showed them pichures to the class." Virgil grinned. "You been wearing a camera about ever since, haven't ya'?"

"Yep." Kevin spit out another seed.

"I guess my cousin Wayne will be takin' a jet trip pretty soon. He went and enlisted."

"He did?"

"Yep. After his leg got healed up, he sold his ATV."

Virgil pulled in his chin and made his voice sound deeper. "Wayne said, 'If I'm gonna git all busted up, I might as well do it defendin' this country!'

"He said he's been thinkin' about it ever since 9/11." Virgil shook his head. "I don't believe him though. He's just playin' the big patriot hero, but that ain't really it. He just can't find no work around here."

"He had him a job in the dollar store. But it was a long drive. Paid crap." Virgil took another bite of melon. "Army'll feed him. He'll git his pichure took in a cool uniform. He'll git to shoot guns. And he won't have to keep on livin' with his parents."

Kevin spit out some seeds. "You think you'll enlist when you get old enough, Virgil?"

Virgil shrugged. "I dunno. Depends, I guess. Might just hang around here and defend my own mama, if I have to."

"I hear ya'."

"Hey, Kevin. Ya' think Jet wants some of this melon rind?"

"Let's give him an end piece. See what he does."

I have to say, the melon was a most refreshing treat. And I did not waste the seeds.

The Report

Changes were in the air. Nights were getting longer, and that meant more danger for me. Dread that a snake could crawl into the coop and devour me kept me awake at night. If a snake got inside, not even Maw could save me.

Kevin was often away all day long. Just at daylight, he always came out to feed me and to do some chores in the barn. But now, on most days, he'd go back to the house and come out wearing different clothes. Then he'd disappear into a big yellow roller.

That kind of roller, I learned, is called a school bus. Like the school bus Virgil had talked about. It took kids away to a place called school—not usually to the doctor's office. In the afternoon, the school bus came back, and Kevin got out. He would change clothes again, and come out to feed me.

Sometimes he brought along things called notebooks. He set them on the picnic table and scratched on them with a sharp yellow stick. Just as he had always done, he took pictures of me.

That routine happened on most days. But on some days, the school bus did not come at all. Kevin was around more then, still giving me speech lessons and scratching on the notebook.

Sometimes he read to me. He did this by looking at his notebook while he talked. He told me he was reading the report he had written about me and other crows. He said he was going to have to read it out loud in science class, so he might as well practice by reading it to me. I found it very interesting.

One afternoon, someone walking with long, quick strides came across the yard. I could tell by his shiny head it was Kevin's father, though he wasn't wearing his usual clothes. His shirt was white. His brown pants matched his unbuttoned jacket, and his necktie flapped in the breeze. "Kevin!" he called before he had reached the coop.

He was holding some white papers. "Son, I just got home from school. Before I left there, Mrs. Gardner stopped me in the hall to speak to me about this science report of yours." He held out the papers. "I guess you know she was pleased. She gave you an A+."

"Yes, Daddy. She said she liked it a lot."

"So does your mother. She just gave it to me to read. Son, I want to tell you how proud we are of you for doing this kind of work. The way you incorporated your pictures of Jet, and your written descriptions of its care and development. Mrs. Gardner said you even showed slides when you gave your presentation to the class."

"Yes. I wanted everyone to see the pictures."

"Well, that was all very good, but you also reported information about the crow species—their range, habitat, diet, and life cycle…It's…It's outstanding work!

"Of course, I know you've always been a capable student, Kevin. But the amount of effort you put into this project is even beyond what I would have expected of a boy your age. It's very impressive!"

"Thank you, Daddy. It was fun for me to raise Jet last summer. I even enjoyed reading everything I could find in the library about crows."

"I can see that bird means a lot to you. Truth to tell, son, when your mama told me you wanted to keep a pet crow, I just wasn't keen on the idea. I thought it might be a distraction. I was wrong.

"Reading this report has shown me that raising that animal has had a good influence on you. I'm glad now that I didn't say no. You made a good choice to keep and study it."

"Thank you, Daddy. I appreciate you letting me raise Jet. But…now I feel confused. I need your advice about something."

"What is it, son?"

The Dilemma

Kevin's forehead wrinkled. "I'm wondering what's the right thing to do now that Jet's grown. I don't know if I should keep it any more."

Kevin's father drew back his head. "I'm surprised you're thinking of turning Jet loose after all the work you've put in. Why, son?"

Kevin sighed and shook his head. "I mean…maybe Jet should be free. Crows are wild animals. Maybe Jet shouldn't be a pet any more."

"Maybe not. But that bird has never been on its own in the wild. Would it survive out there?"

"I'm not really sure."

"Has taking care of Jet become a burden now that you have school along with farm chores?"

"Oh, no! I look forward to coming out here every day and spending time with Jet."

"You know, Kevin, when I was a bit older than you are, I raised a calf to show at the county fair."

"That was old Flora, wasn't it?"

"Yes. She was my project. Oh, I worked so hard with her, and I was just sure she was gonna win me a ribbon. Gollybum, was I disappointed! I felt like I'd wasted my time with her.

"Yet, when time came 'round for my daddy to sell calves, I pleaded with him to let me keep her. When I thought about not having Flora any more, I realized that I was attached to her. Even if she hadn't lived up to my expectations, she was still special to me.

"And so she's still here. And I still enjoy her being here. I'm wondering if you're just disappointed because Jet never learned to talk."

"It really isn't that, Daddy. I know I would surely miss Jet. I just can't seem to make up my mind about what's best now. Is keeping Jet in a cage forever the right thing to do?"

"Well… I think that's a decision you need to make for yourself, Kevin. Maybe you should pray on it."

"Yes, sir. I will, Daddy. Thanks." Kevin nodded. He changed the subject. "Speakin' about Flora made me think about that old house out there above the creek. Virgil and I call it 'Flora's house'. It's about to cave in, isn't it?"

Kevin's father laughed. "Yes, I guess Flora's the lady of the house. It is about to collapse. You know, your great, great granddaddy built that house for his family. All the girls grew up and married and moved off. Later on, the farm was supposed to be split between my daddy and his brother.

"After they both came home from the war, my daddy built this brick house closer to the road for his family. It was more modern. Uncle Ross wanted to go to work in Detroit, so he sold Daddy his half of the farm.

"When my sister and I inherited this place, I bought her half of the farm. Irene had married and moved to Pittsburgh, so she didn't want it.

"That old homeplace had been neglected for a long time, and it wasn't worth fixin' up. Old Flora likes it though."

Kevin laughed. "She sure does! If I don't see her in the pasture, I always know where to look."

"Neither she nor the old house can last much longer, I reckon. I'm gonna miss them both when they're gone. But ya' know what? We're gonna' miss supper if we stay out here all evening."

They walked away side by side. Over Kevin's shoulders, his daddy's arm rested. It was kind of like he had Kevin under his wing, the way Maw used to keep brother and me. I felt jealous.

Kevin's daddy was proud of him for making a good report on me and other crows. I had been studying Kevin and other Persons very closely. If could make a good report on everything I had learned about them, maybe my Maw would be proud of me.

Jet's Report

It wouldn't have pictures, and I couldn't scratch it in a notebook. But I could organize all the information I had collected and give Maw a report on my observations. I set my mind to work on it. I stayed awake all night thinking about it.

The next morning, as soon as Kevin left, Maw came. She dropped a worm into the coop. I gobbled it up.

"Maw, please don't leave right away. I have something important for you."

"What is it, Darling?"

"I've been studying all the Persons who live here or visit here. I'm ready to give you a report on what I've learned. Please listen."

"Certainly."

"This report is based on my personal experiences. Having lived most of my life among Persons, I have had the opportunity to carefully observe a single family of Persons, the Ramseys, as well as their associates.

"Let me begin by defining what are Persons. Persons are a species of animal that is identifiable by five distinctive traits. Those are (1) mode of movement, (2) mode of communication, (3) type of habitat, (4) appearance, and (5) behaviors.

1. MOVEMENT: Persons have unique movement abilities. While most are capable of walking or running upright on their hind legs, they much prefer to roll whenever possible in containers on wheels. They have a wide range of these vehicles for transporting themselves and their belongings. These devices have various purposes and numbers of wheels. Although most animals refer collectively to them as "rollers," Persons have special names for each different kind. For example:

car

bicycle

truck

tractor

ATV

riding mower

wagon

roller skate

skateboard

train

school bus

van

wheelbarrow

Some of these vehicles may be operated by youngsters, but others are for use by mature Persons only. Mothers sometimes place their babies into 'strollers' to accustom them to rolling. Persons are not born with the ability to walk on two legs. They acquire this skill only after learning to walk on all fours.

2. COMMUNICATION: Although other creatures understand the Language of All Beings, Persons seem to forget

it as they learn to use words instead. A baby Person does not have the facility of spoken words. I speculate that they must acquire it over time, by listening carefully and observing, as I have done. They also use facial expressions, gestures, vocal tone, and body posture. However, unlike most other animals, they seem to have limited skill in interpreting nonverbal cues. They have almost no intuition. They rely heavily on words to indicate and describe every object, action, feeling, sound, texture, color, flavor, animal, plant, or substance as well as all parts and combinations of any of those things. Persons are so skilled in word use that they can make marks on paper to represent words. Later, they can speak those same words by looking at the marks. I have observed that some can also represent words by making marks on cake with icing.

3. HABITAT: Persons construct most of their habitat using shapes that have four straight sides. These shapes are called squares and rectangles. They are often joined to form new shapes called boxes or cubes. Regardless of the material from which items are constructed, these shapes are predominant in the surroundings of Persons. For instance, the dwelling space, or house, is a box. The outer walls of the house are made of bricks, which are rectangles. Inside the house, boxes called rooms contain many squares and rectangles. These include doors, windows, window shades, ceilings, floors, rugs, beds, tables, pictures, desks, bookshelves, books, light switches, and floor registers. Persons also keep their tools, large equipment, and pets inside containers of these same shapes.

4. PHYSICAL APPEARANCE: Individuals vary greatly

within the species. Because Persons have no feathers and very little hair, they cover their bodies with clothing. Clothing items may be different depending on the Person's gender, age, preferences, weather conditions, and group identity. Persons also have a wide range of configurations for their hair. It seems that age is a factor in the appearance of a Person's hair. For instance, very young babies and some older males have only a small amount of thin hair on their heads. Older adults may have hair of gray color, though I have not observed this coloration in younger Persons. There are gender differences as well. Adult males sometimes grow long facial hair. Females of any age are more likely than males to wear ornaments in their hair. In both sexes, hair comes in several different shades, as does skin color.

5. BEHAVIOR: Feeding behaviors may occur inside or outside the house. Persons eat some kinds of foods by pushing them into the mouth with their hands. Tools are used for eating other kinds of foods. Mothers use a tool, rather than their own mouth, to place food into the mouths of their babies. Persons prefer to apply heat to many of their foods, but will eat some foods that are cold. Persons with whom I have experience live in small family groups. Bonded pairs are referred to as "married." The male in a pair is called a "husband" and the female is a "wife."

"Limitations of this study: I have been unable to observe house building or mating behaviors. I am also unable to describe the color or size of their eggs. Due to my confinement and inability to read library materials, I have very limited information about the number, range, and distribution of Persons.

"This concludes my report on this unique and interesting species."

I paused and waited. I hoped Maw would be impressed by my accomplishment. I wanted her to say she was proud of me.

Instead, she said, "Well done!"

"Thank you, Maw. Did you really like it?"

"It was very informative. You put a great deal of thought into it."

"But are you proud of me now?"

"Oh, no."

"No? But… but… isn't it better than you would expect of a crow my age? I hoped you would be proud of me."

"Dear One, I will never be proud of you or ashamed of you. You have my everlasting love, and I am deeply grateful for you. That is all."

My heart swelled. "Oh, Maw," I said. "That is all I need."

A Sign

"Hey, Jet, I got a treat for ya." Kevin lowered his head and stepped through the door of the coop with a can of sardines. "I got these special for ya'. They're unsalted and packed in water," he told me as he dropped a small fish into my gaping mouth.

"This is a special day, Jet. Today, we're gonna go up Charry Ridge." Slowly, he fed me four more sardines. Then he scooped me up with his right hand and held me in the crook of his arm against his chest.

I squirmed a little, but with one finger, he tenderly stroked the top of my head. That felt nice. So I got still and closed my eyes. He blew softly on my feathers. "Your down is all gone now. You got your flight feathers. Tail is still a little short, but you're just about all grown up."

He stopped talking for a while. He breathed in and then out slowly. "I've been prayin', like Daddy said, about what to do with you. I think I got an answer this mornin' in church. Our preacher spoke on Matthew 6:26. It says 'Look at the birds of the air; they neither sow nor reap nor gather into barns, and yet your Heavenly Father feeds them.' I feel like that was a sign to me."

Baloney, I thought! When brother and I were starving in our nest, nobody named 'Heavenly Father' ever gave us anything to eat!

Kevin set me on the grass and said, "I'll be right back." I hoped he would be right back with more treats. Instead, he returned with that danged puppy crate!

Oh, no! Not that again! I was hopping mad, so I hopped and flapped and cawed as loud as I could. No use. Kevin caught me in both hands, put me inside the crate, and latched the door. I was trapped again. This time the crate seemed smaller than it had before.

Kevin lifted the crate and set off walking. It was a long way, and being carried in the crate was even bumpier than riding in the backpack. But at least from the crate I could see where we were going. As Kevin climbed the steep hillside, there was less grass. There were more trees, and the trees stood closer together.

It got cooler and darker. Only spots of sunshine reached us. The air smelled different. It was familiar, complex, transcendent. Yes, yes! I recognized this fragrance. It was the breath of Owenasa!

Sweet Sorrow

When Kevin stopped climbing the steep side of the ridge, he set the crate down and opened it. He took a tool from his pocket, and lifted me out of the crate. Holding me firmly against his chest, he used the tool to clamp a thin piece of shiny metal around my right leg.

Once the ring was secure, Kevin stroked my feathers tenderly. His heart seemed to be pounding. So was mine. He said quietly, "You're a big bird now, Jet. I hope you can make it out here on your own. If you get scared or you can't find enough food, you can always come back. I'm gonna..." His voice broke. "I'm gonna miss you." He set me gently on the ground and let go.

I did not trust Kevin to really turn me loose. I was sure he would change his mind, grab me, and stuff me into that crate again. I stayed motionless for several moments. Then I walked a few feet away and waited to see what Kevin would do.

I went a little farther and stopped again. Kevin did not try to catch me. I glanced around at the branches of nearby trees, searching for somewhere to land. Someplace low enough for me to get to, but higher than Kevin could reach, in case he had second thoughts. I spotted a nearby pine with low limbs that were bare and fairly parallel to the ground.

I chose one branch as my target, and decided to go for it. I bent my knees and crouched low. Unfolding my wings, gathering as much air as possible under them, I leaped high. I pushed down hard with my wings and drew my feet up to my chest. Flap, flap, flap.

Flying was difficult, but I was desperate to get away, so I pushed the air under me with all my might. I reached out again and gathered more air. Leaning forward, I fanned my tail feathers. I felt my flight feathers dragging against the air. I was not falling. I was rising! I was getting closer to the tree and farther from Kevin.

I didn't dare look back to see if he was chasing me. I focused on the landing area and stretched my legs toward it. I caught the branch and wrapped my toes around it as tightly as I could. The branch was firm and didn't sag under my weight.

I wobbled forward and back a little, but I used my wings and tail to catch my balance. When I felt steady, I folded my tail and pressed my wings close to my sides. I settled onto my feet, and lowered my head. My heart was beating fast and loud. I hoped he couldn't hear it. I hoped he couldn't see me.

Then just a little above and behind my perch, I heard a voice.

Escape

"Well done, Darling!" It was Maw. She whispered, "Quiet. I followed Kevin here. Now, you follow me."

She flew to a green bough that was a little higher in a nearby pine. I flapped my way up to it. Then she flew to an oak tree, and I caught up with her.

"You're doing fine," she said. She flew to a wild cherry tree and waited. Each time I caught the branches I felt a little more confident. She seemed to be leading me in a circle, but it was only a half circle. When we stopped in the sixth tree, she perched close to me and said, "Stay quiet. Watch him."

There, a short distance downhill from us was Kevin. His head was tilted up. He was searching the trees in the direction where I had first flown. He raised his binoculars to his eyes. He searched some more, in the wrong direction. He's still after me, I thought.

Kevin lowered the binoculars. His shoulders slumped. Suddenly, he dropped to his knees and pressed his hands together. He bowed his head.

"Heavenly Father," he said.

I couldn't see who he was talking to.

"I hope I've done the right thing. Lord, your eye is on the sparrow, and I know you're watching me. I ask that you also watch over this young crow, who is your own creation. I humbly place Jet in your hands now. Amen."

"Oh, no!" I thought. "I don't want Heavenly Father getting his hands on me! He's been spying on some poor sparrow. Now he's going to be watching me, and I can't even see him! Maybe he's made himself small enough to fit into a jet."

Giving a little hop, Maw turned around and faced the opposite way. "Look over here," she whispered.

2

Safety

Return to Owenasa

I turned my head. Behind us, not far uphill from Kevin, was a girl. There was a red stick in her long yellow hair. She was hiding behind an ash tree, watching Kevin. Was she afraid of him, too?

Kevin began carrying the empty crate back down the mountain. He didn't seem to notice the girl, and she did not speak to him. As soon as he was a safe distance away, Maw and I returned to the branch where my parents had built our nest.

Owenasa greeted me. "Welcome home. I have waited long for you, Beloved One."

"A boy named Kevin captured me and tried to make me talk. Then he changed his mind and brought me back."

"I know. How was it for you to live among Persons?"

"Well, they took care of me, but they kept me in a coop. I didn't want to live in a coop." I shook my head. "I wanted to fly, and to be with Maw, and to be with you. You both love me."

"Kevin loved you, too."

"How do you know?"

"He was responsible for you, and he returned the freedom that belonged to you."

"He gave me a wedding ring, too. See?" I held up my leg to show the band Kevin had put there. "Something to remember him by, I guess."

"Something he can recognize you by. He will long to see you again."

"Well, he'd better not catch me again! I belong here with my family."

"That is true."

"Owenasa, I saw a girl in the woods. Her hair is yellow. She has a red stick in it."

"Ashley".

"Yes. Ash tree. She was hiding from Kevin behind an ash tree."

"No. Not 'ash tree'. Ashley. Ashley Belle Morgan. That's her name. She's been coming up Charry Ridge since she was very young. Her family lives on one side of the Ridge, and the Ramsey's farm is on the other side. Ashley has a little sister named Katelyn.

"Ashley comes every day, unless she or someone in her family is sick. She carries food up here for the animals. She brings cans of cracked corn, jars of peanuts, salt blocks, oats, and boxes of raisins. Sometimes she has sunflower seeds, blueberries or apples."

"Why does she do it?"

"Ashley loves animals and wants to understand them. She draws pictures of them, and writes about them in her notebooks."

"Kevin wrote about me in a notebook, too! He didn't draw pictures, though. He made those with a camera. Is Ashley trying to catch the animals?"

"Oh, no. She never tries to touch them. She just watches and listens. She's harmless, so no one fears her, and no one harms her."

"Owenasa, I learned so much when I was among the Persons. But I missed so much. Maw brought me news of the world. She told me about the blossoming of service trees, apples, and wild cherries. She told me of waterfalls and meadows of wildflowers; of sunsets and moonrises and rainbows. I missed all of that."

"Now you will have freedom and chances to learn. You will perfect your skills and make new acquaintances among the creatures of the mountains. But for the moment, sit close to me, Dear One, and rest."

I put my head under my wing. I was safe and unworried. I slept.

Flora

My Maw stayed close. She preened my feathers. She fed me, taught me how to hunt for food, and cautioned me about those who might hunt for me. She shared knowledge I couldn't live without.

For lessons with Maw, I was always eager. With me, she was always patient. Every day, we practiced flying. At first, I observed Maw. Flying in bright sunshine, her feathers flashed white, black, white, black.

Then we flew together. I practiced changing direction, altitude, and speed. I learned maneuvers such as collision avoidance, takeoffs from the ground, and takeoffs from branches and roofs. I learned to handle changes in wind direction and velocity, and how to manage flight during wet weather conditions. I practiced landing. Again and again.

How sublime to have vision unlimited by walls of a room, a crate, a coop, or even the leafy branches of trees! From below the clouds I could see far. Flying above the clouds, I could see even farther; but then there was not much to see.

At last I was flying solo. One crisp morning not a cloud was in view. The sky held only a dazzling ball of radiance. And me.

Below, a stream flowed out from under the trees on the edge of the woods. It turned this way and that, as if it couldn't decide which way to run. I could hear it splashing over rocks as it threw glints of light back up to the sun. I wondered where the water was heading in such a hurry. So just for fun, I flew high above it, twisting and winding along its course.

Far below, in and along the stream, I saw a group of black animals. From high in the sky, it appeared to be a murder of crows. I flew lower to get a better look. They were definitely not crows!

They were the largest animals I had ever seen. They had four legs, long tails, and large heads with ears that protruded from the sides. They were singing a deep, somber song.

Then I spotted a house I had not seen before. The walls leaned, the roof sagged, and some of the siding was missing.

Thick vines grew up the stone chimney. One of the animals was standing inside with its big head sticking out the window.

I was curious about these creatures, so I decided to perch near the one in the house and get acquainted. "Splendid day, isn't it?" I said.

The animal's eyes were half closed, and it chewed a while before responding. "For some."

"I'm uh… just trying to get acquainted with some of my new neighbors," I explained.

It chewed some more before saying, "The neighbors aren't new. You are."

"Yes. Right. Um…those animals over there in the stream. I haven't seen any like them before. Can you tell me what they are?"

"Cows."

"Oh. And are you yourself a cow?"

"I am."

"And is this your house?"

"I've been here for many, many, many seasons. Once the porch roof collapsed, I was able to walk over it and in through the hole where the side door used to be."

"Oh! I think I've heard of you! Is your name Flora?"

She chewed. "Persons call me that."

"The other cows seem to be singing."

"They are."

"It's a sad song, isn't it?"

"They are sad because their baby calves were just taken away. They will never see them again."

"How awful!" I said. "I'm so sorry. I was once taken away from my mother. But we are back together again."

"Your mother is fortunate."

I thought of my brother, but did not mention him. "I am fortunate," I said. "What happened? Why were the calves taken away?"

"When the calves are half-grown, a truck comes dragging a huge head behind it. In the meadow it stops. The head opens its mouth. Men feed the calves into the head. Its jaw slams shut. The truck and head roll away. The cows begin to sing The Song of the Childless Mothers. It's a song of longing—wordless, universal, and ancient.

"How old is it?"

"Old as blood."

"Don't you sing with the other cows?"

"Often in the past I have sung that song. Now it echoes in the hollows of my heart."

She closed her eyes and chewed some more. I supposed she was listening. Quietly as I could, I slipped back into the sky.

Brothers

In a shagbark hickory tree near the pasture fence, I found a fine place to rest in the shade. On the ground a squirrel was busily digging holes and patting them closed. Maw had told me not to get too friendly with those creatures.

Oh, sure, squirrels are cute, clever, and funny. But they can be troublesome for birds during nesting season. I knew he was burying nuts, and that he had a plan for finding them again later.

I could remember where they were, too. All I had to do was recall three nearby landmarks—for example a fence post, a sassafras sapling, and a rock. With those points fixed in my mind, I was sure I could find the buried treasures as easily as that squirrel could. Since squirrels don't mind raiding birds' nests, I thought I wouldn't mind coming back sometime to raid that fellow's cache.

It wasn't windy at all, but the branch I was sitting on suddenly jerked down. I joggled like a fumbled football, but managed to regain my balance. Looking down, I saw two creatures who were looking up at me with enormous dark eyes.

One of them apologized. "Oh, so sorry about that."

I was still a bit shaken. "Why the Sam Hill were you yanking the branch? Good thing I can fly now! I had a terrible fall from a tree when I was younger."

The other one said, "We didn't mean to upset you. We didn't even see you there. We were just browsing on the lower twigs. If we had wings, like you, we'd be nibbling the tips off all the branches up there. Tips are the tenderest and best."

These creatures stood on four long, slender legs. They had short brown hair and slim, pointed faces. Their huge ears stuck out of their heads—sort of like the cows' ears.

The tops of their heads were most interesting. The smaller one had two lumps between his ears. The bigger animal had short, fuzzy branches growing out of his head. As they turned to walk away, I saw them twitch their tails.

"Wait a minute!" I cawed after them. They stopped and looked back. Maw had told me about whitetail deer. She said they are big, but not predators. I thought these might be them.

"Are you two whitetails?"

"Yes," said the larger one with the mossy sticks on his head. "I'm called Juniper, and this is my little brother, Dewy."

"I'm called Jet. I've heard of you bucks. Maw says you are friends of Ashley."

"That's right. She gave us our names. She's been friends with our mama since before we were born. She calls our mama Farah. What's that thing on your leg?"

I knew he meant the band Kevin had put on me. "Long story. A boy gave it to me. He also gave me my name. If you don't mind my asking, why are you wearing branches on your head."

Dewy laughed. "Branches. If Juniper had branches on his head, I'd eat them off."

Juniper stamped his foot at him. "Actually, these are called antlers. Only bucks have them. Does don't get any. Dewy is a recent arrival, so he only has knobs this time. He'll get a pair of real antlers when he's full-grown."

"Very handsome," I said. "And are those purely decorative?"

"Not really. Status mostly. But we can also defend ourselves with them, if necessary," Juniper explained.

I thought it would be futile to fight with such dull weapons. Better to have sharp teeth, poisonous venom, some razor-like claws, or at least a powerful stench.

Not having any external ears of my own, I was fascinated by the ears of other animals. I noticed that all the while we were talking, the whitetail brothers were moving their ears. The ears moved independently forward or back, as if each had a mind of its own. I asked why they were doing that.

"Got to be vigilant," said Dewy. "Don't want anything sneaking up on us."

Juniper added, "We are constantly listening. We don't really see all that well—especially in daylight. But our hearing and smell alert us to approaching dangers. You know, like rolling machines, hunting Persons, bobcats, coyotes, and dogs."

Dewy shivered. "Oooh, dogs! Dogs are the worst. They aren't even hungry, but they'll chase us until we are exhausted. If we aren't fast enough to get away, they'll bite us just to be mean."

"He's right. They literally hound us to death in the woods. Dewy is still sort of puny, so I stick close to him. I keep my eye on him when Mama isn't around. Besides, he's a lot of fun to play with."

"I understand," I said, remembering my own big brother and how he had tried to look out for me.

Dewy sniffed the air. "Speaking of Mama, Juniper, shouldn't we meet up with her? I think she's not far away."

"Sure. You're right." Juniper raised his nose and sniffed the breeze. "In the trees just across the brook down there. Better check in. Nice to meet you, Jet."

"See you around," I said.

In an elegant arc, Juniper leaped high over the barbed wire fence, and dashed across the meadow through the tall patches of purple ironweed and bright goldenrod. Dewy followed. White tails up and away!

Race

Ever so gradually the grasses and trees were changing colors, as Maw had told me they would. The greens of meadow grasses and leafy trees faded. They were being replaced by amber, orange, crimson, maroon, and vermillion.

Each day I drifted above the treetops marveling at the colorful array. I would choose a color and perch in a tree of that hue.

While sunlight glowed through their leaves I enjoyed many a pleasant chat with river birches, red maples, tulip poplars, wild cherries, hickories, walnuts, elms, and oaks. The trees were delighting in the attention of many visitors—Persons who came to admire, and animals who came looking for food.

One afternoon, while snacking on fruit in a black tupelo, I spotted a white plume streaming up from the edge of the sky. At the top of that streak a point of light gleamed. I knew it was a jet!

I had heard Kevin say that a crow is fast like a jet. I was sure I was faster. I would challenge that jet to a race and beat it! It was headed toward a tall oak tree on the far edge of the sky. I chose that tree as the finish line. To be fair, I waited for the jet to be straight above me, so we would have an equal start.

When the jet was directly over my head, I launched myself into the air and flew faster than I ever had. Fortunately, the wind was with me. It was a long way to travel, and it took all the strength I had to maintain my speed.

I perched on a branch high in the oak tree at the end of the race. The jet still sparkled in the sky far behind me, nowhere near the tree yet. I watched its tail grow longer and longer.

"I won! I won! I won!" I announced, pulsing my wings. I stopped my victory chant when I looked beyond the place where I had landed. I saw splendor! Another vast expanse of variegated treetops spread out before me. And far, far off, another edge of the sky!

Beneath me, several cars were parked on a roadside lot. Persons were standing or sitting near the cars. Many had cameras or binoculars. All were gazing at the marvelous view. As far as it was possible to see, there was forest. Only forest and sky. I knew this must be the special place Maw had told me about. It was the Blue Ridge Parkway!

Far below, at the bottom of a ravine, I could hear water flowing, but I couldn't see it through the rhododendron bushes. I was hot and thirsty after my race. So I flew down to get a cool drink and to rest my aching wings.

Kits

As I landed, I was surprised to see an animal on the other side of the stream. It looked a bit like me I thought. It had a pointy face with brown eyes surrounded by black, just as mine are. Like me, it had toes. But it had five, and I have only four.

It had four legs instead of two and fur instead of smooth feathers. Its tail was fluffy with light and dark rings on it. The animal was patting the mud at the water's edge.

Then it did an astonishing thing. It pulled a small crawdad out of the mud. Standing on its hind legs, it started eating its catch.

It saw me watching, and snarled, "What are you staring at?"

"I was just wondering what what you're doing. Were you washing your food just now?" I asked.

"Was I washing my …? Humph! What a ridiculous question!" It shook its head. "Of course not!"

"Well, what were you doing?"

"I was finding my food, silly. Our front paws are very sensitive, especially under water; so we can feel where food might be hiding in the stream bed."

We? Who is this "we" that has such sensitive paws, I wondered.

"What kind of animal are you?" I asked.

It gulped down its last mouthful of food. "What kind of...? What kind of feather brain are you? I'm a raccoon! Don't you know anything?" it growled.

"I know quite a lot, actually. But you see, I fell out of my nest when I was a chick. A boy captured me. He took me to his house and kept me locked up. Then he changed his mind and turned me loose. So other than some Persons, I haven't yet met many animals. Just one cow and two deer."

The raccoon dropped back onto all fours, stretched its neck toward me, and tilted its head. "Oh, you poor, poor thing! Having to live among those rascals. No wonder you're so ignorant. Persons can be very destructive, you know. Sorry I snapped at you. I didn't know you'd just gotten out of captivity."

"No harm," I told her.

"Listen, I'd like to chat more, but I have to get back to my den and feed my kits. If you'd like to come along, I'll introduce you to my family."

"I'd like that very much. Thanks!"

"Just follow me," she said. "Hurry. I know they'll be hungry."

I was surprised by her speed. Although I'm fast in the sky, keeping up with mama raccoon was a challenge in the dense undergrowth. I hardly had room to spread my wings.

Luckily, her home was not far away. She stopped at a vine-covered, half-dead tree with a great hole near the bottom of its trunk.

"I'm going inside. Meet me up there." She pointed with her nose to indicate another hole about half-way up the trunk.

In she dashed. I flapped my way up until I reached the opening. I perched there just as her head popped out.

"Kits!" she called. "We have a visitor."

Four little faces poked out of the opening. They looked a bit like me, except... well, no. Actually, they looked just like her. Cute!

The kits all began chattering at once.

Raccoon tried to introduce me. "This is my new friend...Uh..."

"They call me Jet. Hello, kits!" I said, trying to be genial.

The kits totally ignored me. They turned to their mother and attacked her belly as ravenously as she had attacked the crawdad! I was shocked.

"Excuse them," their mama explained. "Once they've finished nursing, they'll be friendlier to you. They're just really hungry right now.

"I got a late start with this litter. Didn't meet my mate until late this breeding season. They're almost weaned."

"The view of the forest from up above is exquisite," I said. "This is my very first visit to the Parkway. I have never seen so far before. I was born blind, and then spent most of my life in confinement, so now I'm eager to see all I can."

"Born blind? Well, there's something we all have in common. I was born blind, too. And it was a long time before my kits opened their eyes or their ears.

"Actually, they are a lot less trouble that way. Soon they'll be into everything. I'll have my paws full trying to teach them and keep them out of mischief."

"What sorts of things will they learn?"

"To begin with, they need to master climbing down this tree trunk. We have a special way to do it—head first; back feet pointing straight up. After that, I'll show them how to use the community latrine.

"They'll need to practice hunting and fishing skills. I'll teach them to scavenge for food around picnic areas. They have to know how to defend themselves from predators. And—to have any chance at all to survive—they must learn to cross roads safely. Speed limits in the park are low, but you know how Persons are."

"That's quite a curriculum! Will your mate help you with teaching?"

"Oh, no. He's a boar. Their daddy won't be around until next breeding season. But we'll be fine. The kits will stay close to me, until I have my next litter.

"The Parkway is a great place to raise young! Lots of good places for dens, plenty of water and food, and no hunters or trappers. Dogs are usually on leashes."

Once the kits had their bellies full of milk, their eyes and ears were on me. To entertain them I told them about my race with the jet. After that, their eyes began to droop. I was tired too, so it was time to leave.

"Now that you have your freedom, what are you going to do next, Jet?" Mama raccoon asked.

"I plan to continue my own education. The world is much larger than I realized. And it's more complex than I ever imagined. Nice meeting you and your family," I said as I turned to go.

"Our pleasure," the raccoon said as she cuddled her drowsy little ones. "Just a word of caution before you go. You and I are friends now. I would never impose on you. But not all raccoons should be welcome visitors in your nest—if you catch my meaning."

"Thanks for the warning." Spreading my wings and giving a hop, I was away to roost for the night.

Mountains

Next morning I was in no hurry to go home. I flew over some of the wide valleys and deep gorges along the parkway. In the air I met several ravens who are better at soaring than I am. Those fellows are masters of the currents.

At times I perched near the overlooks along the road and listened to conversations of the Persons. Many had come from faraway places to stand in awe before the beauty of these mountain forests.

When I returned home, Owenasa welcomed me. "I just had the most exalting experience!" I told her. "Though I was standing still in a treetop, I felt I was gliding above the earth."

"You've been to the Parkway."

"Yes! How did you know?"

"It affects everyone that way."

"I had no idea that the real edges of the sky were so far away."

"The edges of the sky are not stitched to the treetops. They are always moving, just like the sky's face."

"Sometimes, I couldn't tell where the blue mountains ended and the sky began. I didn't know that the mountains were so vast. Do they go on forever?"

"These mountains stand far to the northeast and to the southwest. But if you travel to where the sun rises, you will see that the mountains lie down before the Ocean."

"What is the Ocean?"

"The Ocean is a place of mighty water. It is older and greater than all the mountains of the world. These mountains we live in are ancient. When they were young, they stood much taller. These are the grandchildren of earlier mountains."

"There were mountains before these mountains?"

"Yes. Mountains came here twice before. The first rose high and mighty, and then they fell down. The Ocean swallowed them up. The next mountains reached almost to the sky. But they also fell into the depths."

"Do you remember when the Ocean was here?"

"Dear One, I am very old, but not even I can recall that. Only the rocks know. The secrets that underlie everything were lifted to the summits, and held by the rocks. The rocks can tell of life when the Ocean was here."

"Could these mountains fall down, Owenasa?"

"Perhaps. Mountains change. Just like the water and just like the sky."

This information was disturbing. I loved these mountains. I wanted them never to change. I became anxious and wanted my Maw. I cawed to her. She answered, and I flew to meet her. I told her what Owenasa had described to me.

"Maw," I said, "I feel afraid again. When I think that the mountains may fall down and the Ocean may gobble us up, I'm anxious. It's hard to breathe and my heart beats fast. I feel just as scared as I did when the hawk attacked, and when Kevin put me in his backpack."

"Darling, perhaps you will feel better if you meet the Ocean face to face."

"Have you met the Ocean, Maw?"

"I have. When cold, dark nights grow long, throngs of crows travel from many places and converge in trees to roost for a while. We roost near the place where the land meets the Ocean and two great roads cross each other. Crows gather there to share information about the weather, food sources, and good places to nest. We play games and some of us find mates. That is where I met your father, may he be fondly remembered. After the roost, he traveled with me to Owenasa to begin our family."

"I'm not sure I'm brave enough to face the Ocean. Not yet."

"As you wish. Let me know if you change your mind. Meanwhile, it may calm you to make some new friends. I don't think you've met the Morgan sisters yet. Follow me. I'll take you to a clearing where Ashley is putting out food and Katelyn is playing."

Gossip

Maw and I perched in a locust tree and watched the girls. I recognized Ashley at once. She was cutting up apples and tossing the pieces here and there. Katelyn looked different from her. She was smaller, and had curly black hair and blue eyes.

Katelyn was busy gathering flattish stones and pieces of litter from the forest floor—sticks of various sizes, leaves, pine cones, turkey tail mushrooms, and curved hunks of mossy bark. She seemed to be examining each piece and choosing only the sizes, shapes, and colors that pleased her. She carried her selections to a place where long ago a tree had lived, died, and shape-shifted into an infinity of complexes.

Only a few remnants were still recognizable as tree parts. There was just a jagged, stump with peeling bark. Its gnarled roots criss-crossed each other in a lumpy network that stretched in every direction.

When she stopped gathering, Katelyn began to assemble her materials into little clusters among hills and valleys of the roots.

At first, I thought she was trying to build a nest. Hers was not too bad an attempt—for a Person.

Ashley approached, crouched, and studied the scene. "Are you still making a fairy house?"

"Oh, this here is a whole fairy village," Katelyn said, stretching out her hands above her creation. "It's not finished yet." Katelyn reached into a pocket of her overalls and took out a handful of pebbles. She carefully placed them throughout her village. "I got these long, long ago when we went to Fairy Stone State Park. I was little, and I used to believe that the fairy stones would turn back into fairies at night. I kept them on the footboard of my bed. I was hopin' I'd wake up before mornin' and see 'em flyin' around in my room." She put one fairy stone back into her pocket. "I'm keepin' this one for good luck."

Ashley walked to a large rock, brushed some dirt from it, and sat. She set a sketchbook on her lap. Out of her hair, she pulled the red stick and began rubbing the point of it on the book. The rubbing made a soft scratchy sound and left black marks on the page. Sometimes the scratches were long, and sometimes they were short and fast.

Without stopping her work, Katelyn said, "Ashley, I want to ask you somethin'."

"Ask."

"Why ain't you popular?"

Ashley chuckled. "I guess you better ask people that don't like me. They're the ones who know."

"I was just wonderin' if you know you ain't popular. 'Cause some people are sayin' you ain't."

"Some people. Is that right?"

"Yeah. You remember Saturday evenin' when we was in town and Granny let you and me git a cone of ice cream while she was jammin' with her music friends?"

"I do. Why?"

"Because when you went to the bathroom, and I was sittin' in the booth by myself, there was two girls sittin' in the booth behind of me. They saw you, but they never seen me. And after you was inside the bathroom, they was sayin' how they know you from school."

"I saw them. That was Lily Pritchard and Connie Fenimore."

"Well, they was sayin' that you are the weirdest girl in school. They said you dress funny, and don't do nothing with your hair but make it in a braid and stick a pencil through it. They said you was named for a doll, so you think you're a living doll. And they said you was too skinny, and nobody wants to sit by you in the cafeteria 'cause you don't eat meat, and our whole family don't go to church nowhere, and you probably are a Communist anyway."

Ashley put her arms across her waist and bent over laughing.

Katelyn stopped what she was doing and stood across from her sister. "Ashley! What's so funny? I was afraid of tellin' you, in case your feelin's would git hurt. I sure didn't think you'd bust out laughin'. Don't you even care if people don't like you?"

"Oh, little sister," Ashley grinned and shook her head. "I surely hope you aren't worryin' yourself over any of this. No. It don't hurt my feelings a bit." Ashley's smile melted. Her eyes searched her sister's face. "Now, Katelyn. I have a question for you. Are you ashamed of me?"

"No! It ain't that! But…I love you, and I want other people to love you and not say bad things about you. I want you to have friends, Ashley."

Ashley took Katelyn's hand in her two hands. "I love you, too. So I'll explain some things about me to you. But you remember," she held up her index finger, "This is just for you. I don't explain myself to people who don't love me. And you don't have to make excuses for anything I do. OK?"

Katelyn nodded.

"First off, about my clothes. I sew all my school dresses. They're simple and comfortable, and I put big patch pockets in front, so I can carry notepads in case I need one. I can slide out of them dresses fast when I get home, and slide right into my overalls.

"I ain't got time to fool around unbucklin' belts, unzippin' zippers, takin' off earrings and bracelets, and wigglin' out of panty hose. I'm in a hurry to git my chores done, so I can come up into these woods and draw and study animals. I ain't no fashion model. I'm a student and an artist.

"Besides, Katelyn, I don't want Granny to spend a lot of money on gittin' me fancy clothes. Some kids think they have to wear clothes with logos on 'em. I don't. Granny knows I'd rather have feed for the animals, seed for the birds, and art supplies instead of designer named outfits.

"I always keep a sharp pencil in my hair, in case I see something I want to sketch. I ain't a Communist or a doll, and we don't go to church 'cause our whole family ain't churchy people. We just believe in the Golden Rule. And we don't believe in makin' a lot of extra rules for other people to follow.

"And I'm skinny, because I'm skinny." Ashley went back to scratching with the red stick that I now knew is called a pencil.

Katelyn brushed dirt off her hands. "Ashley," she asked, "are you mad at them girls now—Lily and Connie—for badmouthin' you?"

"Not at all. It's a free country." She shrugged. "People got a right to not like me, and they got a right say so—behind my back or in front of my face. And if I choose not to care about it, that's my right."

Katelyn sat on a moss-padded rock across from her sister. She placed an elbow on her knee and made a fist for her chin to rest on. She was quiet for a little while, gazing into the tree tops. "But, Ashley…" she hesitated. "Ya know…I do want people to like me."

Ashley stopped scratching with the pencil. "There's nothin' wrong with wantin' that, Katelyn. But just don't try too hard to get everyone to like you."

"Why not?"

Ashley started the pencil scratching again. "Because, you could be givin' others the power to turn you into someone you don't like."

"Kinda like black magic then? Right?"

Ashley made a sort of coughing sound that I think was a kind of laugh. She poked the pencil back into her hair and said. "Sort of, I guess. How's this?" She showed Katelyn the notepad she was scratching on. It had black marks all over it now.

Katelyn took it with both hands. She looked it over and said, "Oh! My! Gosh! Ashley, this is beautiful! You sketched my fairy village. You even drew some fairies in it! I think your pencil is magic!" She pressed the notepad to her chest. "I'm gonna keep this picture forever!"

Ashley smiled, pulled the pencil out of her hair, and handed it to Katelyn. "Here. Now you have a magic pencil for writing your stories and songs."

Katelyn accepted the pencil and rolled it between two fingers and thumb. She looked up at her sister. "Ashley, when I'm a grown-up famous author, will you make the pictures for my books?"

Ashley's dark eyes twinkled, "I'd be pleased to." Ashley picked up her backpack, slipped her arms through the straps, and started down the path toward home. "Come on now. We need to git back and help Granny. What's for supper this evenin'?"

"We're havin' collards, pintos, and corn bread with fried apple pies for dessert. I made the pies."

"I love your fried pies, Katelyn! And I love Granny's collards. She's the only one I know that makes them good without any pig fat."

"Hey! That reminds me. When you was explainin' yourself, you never did say why you won't eat meat."

"Oh, yeah… well, that's a story for another day."

A Line of Questions

Maw was right. Being near the Morgan girls had a calming effect on me. I wasn't nervous around them as I was with Kevin. They took my mind off tumbling mountains and that ravenous monster, the Ocean.

I started watching the sisters in the woods on Charry Ridge. I liked snacking on the cracked corn and peanuts Ashley set out.

By listening to the girls talk to each other, I learned new words. Now and then I followed them home. I happened to be there one laundry day.

I noticed that Katelyn had a special way of moving from place to place sometimes. She would extend her arms over her head, then place her hands on the ground. While her hands were down, she'd lift one leg and then the other straight up, so she was standing briefly on her hands. Her curly head was hanging between her arms. Next, she'd put one foot and then the other back on the ground.

She could do this over and over, so that she seemed to roll like a wheel. As I watched her doing this one day, an adult female with gray-streaked hair came out of the house carrying a big basket.

"When you're done cartwheelin', would you mind helpin' me to hang some laundry on the line?"

"Sure, Granny! I'll cartwheel right over to ya'."

The Granny set down the basket and handed Katelyn a plump bag. "Here, just hand me a pin as I need one."

"Yes, ma'am."

Granny took a wet, wadded shirt from the basket and shook it. It went pop. She turned it and pinned it to the line. The arms of the shirt hung down and waved in the breeze.

She did the same with three more shirts and two of Ashley's dresses. She pinned five pairs of overalls by their legs. I wondered if Katelyn did cartwheels to let her clothes practice being upside down.

While the clothes were being pinned to the line, Katelyn was asking questions and Granny was answering them.

"Granny, how's come we don't eat meat like ever body else around here? I asked Ashley once, but she never did answer me."

"Oh, honey. It just upsets your sister, so I cook other things. There's plenty to eat around here—vegetables, herbs, corn, eggs."

"And berries, grapes, apples, nuts, honey, pears, and mushrooms."

"Right. So we ain't goin' hungry without meat on the table, are we?"

"No. But why does eatin' meat bother Ashley so?"

"Well, when she was younger than you are now, your daddy was about to send her up here to live with us. But first, they went to say their good-byes to your mama's family over in West Virginia. Your Granny Jean took your daddy and Ashley to your mama's Aunt Nelda. Now, your mama's Aunt Nelda is the sister to your mama's daddy, ya see?

"I see."

"Nelda had a little plot of land, and she raised her a garden and kept a couple of goats and some chickens. Well, Ashley loved to pet and play with them biddies while the grownups was talkin'.

"Your daddy said that, it bein' Sundee, Aunt Nelda decided she'd fix a fried chicken supper. She walked over to where Ashley was playin'. Nelda picked up a hen and wrung its neck right there. Dead chicken went to hoppin' all around and fallin' over.

"Ashley never had seen nothin' like that. Your daddy said she just stiffened up and screamed and screamed. He said he couldn't hardly git her to settle herself down.

"He said she cried so she couldn't catch her breath. Needless to say, she didn't eat no chicken supper that day."

"I never seen nothin' like that neither. It sounds horrible! Why'd Aunt Nelda do that?"

"Just because that's the way a lot of country people do. They don't think no more of that than a cat thinks of catchin' a mouse. Some people don't go to the supermarket and buy a package of meat. They raise animals for food, and when they want, they kill them.

"Anyway, your daddy told me Ashley said she wouldn't never eat meat again. He didn't try to force her, and I don't neither."

"Okay, then. I don't care what the other kids think. Our family don't eat meat. And that's that."

Sweet Tea

Under the weight of the wet laundry, the clothesline sagged. Granny propped up the middle of each line with a pole. They rocked in the breeze, back and forth like metronomes that couldn't keep a beat. She picked up the empty basket and went back into the house.

Katelyn cartwheeled away. She stopped and looked back, watching the clothes. She waved her hands as if they were drifting like leaves on the wind. Her lips moved. Then she started to speak:

Upside down clothes,

Flappin' in the sky,

Do you wish that you could fly?

Upside down clothes

Make a nice design.

Some are Ashley's, some are mine.
Upside down clothes,
Hangin' out to dry
Sayin' hello or wavin' good-bye?

She put her hands on her hips and said, "Someday, I'm gonna' grow that into a song." She cartwheeled over to the porch and sat down on the bottom step.

Ashley came out with a sweaty glass in each hand. "You been out in the sun for a while. Want some sweet tea?"

"You bet I do!"

Ashley sat by her sister and handed her a drink. Katelyn took a big gulp. "Ashley, do you think people that eats meat are evil?"

"No, I do not. It's not my business what other people eat. I choose what I eat, and I suppose others want to choose for themselves. Why?"

"Because…well, it means that animals are gonna get killed for their food. That's a sin, ain't it?"

Ashley sipped her tea. "Katelyn, lots of animals kill and eat other animals. Coyotes will kill a deer and eat it. Hawks will kill and eat doves. That doesn't make them evil. Some animals, like deer and rabbits and cows just eat vegetation. They aren't better than the other animals. Right? Each kind just follows its own way.

"The only thing I think is wrong is when people are cruel to animals—make them live in crowded, filthy places. Kill them in ways that make them suffer fear and pain.

"Everything that lives has to die sometime. I just think humans should respect other animals. If they're going to take an animal's life, they should be merciful how they do it."

Ashley gently turned Katelyn's face toward hers. "If you feel like you want to try eatin' meat, you don't need my permission. It's your choice. I just don't want nothin' to lose its life for my sake."

"Me neither!" Katelyn said. She chugged down the last of her tea. "I'm gonna do some more cartwheels now."

"Does having your head upside down help you think?"

Katelyn stuck out her tongue.

Fiddle Sticks

I flew to the Morgan farm the next day, hoping that Katelyn would be outside. Before I arrived, I could hear music. But this music was not the singing of cows. It was not the singing of birds. This new kind of music floated up from the valley in which the Morgan house stood on its stone foundation.

The Morgans lived in a white two-story house with a shiny roof and a stone chimney at each end. Out front, Granny and Katelyn were sitting on long benches. Under their chins, they were holding wooden boxes with long handles. Each also held a stick that she dragged across the wooden thing. Back and forth. That's where the music came from!

I perched on the rail of the upper level porch and listened. I had never heard anything like it. The music made me want to move. I bobbed my head, pulsed my wings, and swayed from side to side.

When the sticks stopped moving, the music stopped. Granny said, "That was good! Now let's try that Kate Long tune. I wanna play it at the Ferrum Folk Life Festival. You know the words, so why don't you sing it, honey?"

Katelyn nodded. Granny tucked her wooden box under her chin again, tapped her foot, and ran the stick across the box. The music started, and Katelyn began to sing a song with words. Her voice was light and pure as the voice of any songbird.

"Leaves are falling and turning in showers of gold,
As the postman climbs up our long hill,
And there's sympathy written all over his face
As he hands me a couple more bills.
Who'll watch the home place?
Who'll tend my heart's dear space?
Who'll fill my empty place,
When I am gone from here?"

When the music finished, Katelyn said, "I love that song, Granny."

"I do too, and you sing it so beautiful, Katelyn."

"Thank you. I'd like to practice 'The Blackest Crow.' This time you sing and I'll play. OK?"

Katelyn put her music box under her chin, and Granny sang these words:

"Each night I suffer for your sake,
You're the one I love most dear.

I wish that I was going with you
Or you were staying here.
The blackest crow that ever flew
Would surely turn to white,
If ever I prove false to you,
Bright day would turn to night."

When the music stopped this time, Granny had a big smile on her face as she said to Katelyn, "That was fine playin'! You are comin' along so well with your lessons!"

"I want to be good enough to play at the Old Fiddlers' Convention someday."

"I'm sure you will do. Alright then, now would you carry these here fiddles and bows into the house? And fetch me a big Mason jar full of water?" Granny handed Katelyn her fiddle and stick.

"You don't want a glass?"

"Naw, honey. Just a jar. There's a two-quart right by the sink."

While Katelyn was inside, Granny went into the shed and got a pair of pruners. From the rose bush at the end of the porch she cut several blossoms. Katelyn returned with the jar, and Granny put the cuttings into the water.

"These will be about the last blooms of this year. Your granddaddy Glenn planted this bush for me when we was first married." She held the jar out to Katelyn.

Katelyn sniffed the blossoms, closed her eyes, and smiled.

"Now, Katelyn, lately you been wantin' to know about your roots. Take a walk with me, and I'll show you where some of them are planted."

Roots

Granny and Katelyn passed through the gate in the rail fence and latched it behind them. They started along a path that curved up to the top of a hill behind the house. I knew where they were headed. The path led to a clearing among some cedar trees. Flat stones stuck up from the ground there.

I flew to the top of one of the cedar trees and waited for them to arrive. As they entered the clearing, Granny said, "You girls have been here before, but then you didn't seem much interested in knowing who was restin' here."

"I know. We was just little. We liked to run around the headstones, and play hide and seek, and sit under these cedars. It's shady and it smells nice there."

"Well, now you can read the stones and ask me any questions you have. I'll tell you all I know."

I wondered if these stones are the ones that Owenasa said could tell about times long ago. But they didn't talk. They could only tell their stories to Persons who could read them.

"There's some really old stones here, and they're kinda hard to read. Does this say 1789?"

"The Morgans has been on this land for many generations. Some of them is graves of men that served in Revolutionary War battles. One had fought in the Battle of Kings Mountain in South Carolina."

"Some of these is babies' graves."

"That's right. In times past, most people had big families. A lot of children didn't live to grow up. A lot of mothers died giving birth."

"Why did the babies die?"

"Lots of reasons. Diseases, accidents, starvation. Wasn't medical care around here like there is now."

Katelyn walked quietly among the stones looking carefully at each one. Granny kneeled in front of a stone and poured a little water from the jar into a hole in the ground. She placed three roses in that hole.

Katelyn came and stood by her. She looked at the stone and said, "Glenn Albert Morgan. May 12, 1948 to November 1, 1967. That's Granddaddy's grave."

"That's right."

"How did he die?"

"There was a war in Vietnam. The government was callin' men to go fight over there. Glenn and I was married in June of 1966, just after we graduated high school. He got drafted into the military November that year. The government wasn't exempting married men or only sons no more. They was takin' about ever body. A year later, Glenn's body come home in a coffin."

"Granny, your name is on this stone too. Alma Lyn Morgan!"

"That's right. When my time is over, that will be my restin' place."

Katelyn looked at the stone beside that one. "Scott Braxton Morgan. Beloved son, husband, and father. And that's my daddy's grave."

"It is."

Katelyn's brow furrowed. "Well, let's see. If Daddy was born in March 1968, and Granddaddy died in November 1967 over in Vietnam, then…my daddy never knew his daddy. Did he?"

"No. Your daddy and his daddy never seen each other in this life." Alma placed three roses in the hole by Scott's stone.

Katelyn moved to another stone. "This one says 'Spencer Cleve Morgan.' Who was he?"

"Well, now, he was your daddy's granddaddy. Spencer helped me raise Scott. My boy thought the world and all of his granddaddy. In World War II, Spencer was a signalman in the Navy. You know that patch we have in a frame hangin' on the wall in the livin' room?"

"Uh-huh. It looks like a bird with two little flags under it."

"Yes. Well, the sailors call that a 'crow'. That was Spencer's signalman's patch from his uniform. He gave that to your daddy. Scott was so proud of it. Spencer used to tell Scott stories about all the places where that crow had traveled during the war. Spencer would show him on the globe where those places are in the world."

"Did Great Grandaddy Spencer ever know me?"

"He did. And you was a special joy to him. He was sick at the time you come here. I worried that a baby cryin' would trouble him. But he said hearin' a young one in the house again made him feel better. He loved to hold you in his rocker and sing to you."

Katelyn studied a stone right beside Spencer's. "This here is Spencer's wife's grave, ain't it? Taisie Scott Morgan. Born March 19, 1926. Died February 5, 1950."

"It is. You know, Taisie sewed them pretty quilts you girls have on your beds. She used cloth from feed sacks to make a lot of them patches. People didn't have money for buyin' fabrics, so they made do with what they had."

"Them quilts are beautiful!"

"A lot of the recipes we cook is Taisie's, too."

"Wait a minute." Katelyn went back to Glenn's grave and looked at the stone again. "Grandpa Glenn was born in 1948. So he was still only a little baby when his mama died."

"That's right. She got cut on a rusty nail. Infection killed her. Spencer raised Glenn mostly by hisself. Then, after raisin' his own son, he helped me to raise mine. I don't know what we'd have done without that kind man." She placed some roses on Spencer and Taisie's graves.

"Taisie's name has the same name as my daddy's in it. Scott."

"Scott was her family name. Glenn wanted his son named in honor of his mama."

"I see." Katelyn paused. "Granny, if my daddy and his daddy and his daddy before him was all veterans, shouldn't there be some flags on their graves?"

"No!" Alma spoke a bit sharply. Then more gently as she explained. "I got one flag when Glenn was killed. All folded in a neat triangle. A dear price was paid for that. I just..." She shook her head. "I don't want no other flags on this place." Alma set her hand on top of the stone to steady herself as she got up.

"Granny, was our family poor people?"

"Well, now that depends on what you mean by 'poor'. If you mean did they have a lot of money to buy things, no they didn't. People grew or hunted or fished for their food. They built or created most of what they needed, and whatever needed mendin' they fixed. They made medicines from what they had growing on the land. Folks even made their own music and dances.

"People traded with others one thing for another. Some things they bought. They really didn't need money for much, except to pay taxes to the government for livin' on their own land.

"Pretty much nothin' got wasted. They made the most out of all they had. If they hadn't, they couldn't have survived. Myself, I don't call people like that poor. I call them resourceful."

"What about your family, Granny? I want to hear about them, too."

"Not much to tell. My parents was wanderers. They was both highly educated and artistic. Daddy liked to paint, and mama wrote poetry. I don't think they meant to have a family. I just sorta happened. I was in and out of schools, but we always had books and read a lot. They come down here and tried to live off the land. But the work was too hard for them, and they had too much money to need to do it. They enrolled me in the high school. That's when I met Glenn."

"Where are they now?"

"I don't know. When I was a senior, a friend of my daddy's come from California to stay with them. Then mama and daddy had a big row. They split up. Daddy went out to San Francisco with his friend. I never did hear from him again. Mama wanted to move back to Brooklyn where she come from. I wanted to stay here with Glenn. So she left me here.

"After my parents went their own ways, one of my teachers fixed it up for me to room with her mama, a kind lady named Mrs. Dwiggins."

"Ain't she the lady you visit at the nursing home?"

"She is. I try to get there once a month. I take her flowers and play some music for her. She can't remember me, but that don't matter. I remember her.

"Mrs. Dwiggins taught me how to use her sewin' machine and helped me make a dress to wear to the prom. I stayed with her til Glenn and I got married. She come with me to the courthouse for our wedding. My bouquet was flowers from her garden. For our wedding gift, she give us pillow cases that she made and embroidered with hearts and birds.

"Well, my mama, a while after she left, she met an old boyfriend of hers. She sent me a postcard from Mallorca once, but it didn't have no return address on it."

"Don't you miss them?"

"I can't say as I do. We was just three people traveling together for a while. Spencer Morgan was more of a father to me than my own daddy ever was. It was him that taught me how to cook and garden and care for my baby. He taught me how to play fiddle, too. He always treated me just like I was his own daughter. I felt like part of the Morgan family, and like I had a home in these mountains."

Katelyn looked around at the grave stones. "Our family's gettin' small. There's a lot more dead people than livin' ones. Granny, do you think my mama is dead, too?"

"Honey, I don't know who knows the answer to that. She was a darlin' girl, she was. Smart and talented. Loved ever body. She would have been a good mama to you and Ashley, if she could have. I do know that."

Alma picked up the empty Mason jar. She and Katelyn silently walked from the place of the graves and down the long path. When they reached the gate, Katelyn took hold of Alma's hand and stopped.

"Granny," Katelyn said. "I'll watch the homeplace." She pressed Alma's hand against her cheek.

The Stranger

The next morning was rainy and dreary. I rested most of the day. By afternoon, the rain had stopped. It was misty. Not a good day for viewing the Parkway. The Morgan girls would be at school. So I decided to fly over town and look for spilled garbage around the green boxes by Cox's Grocery Store.

As I was pecking into a bag of stale buns, a school bus stopped. Its doors folded open, and three kids jumped out. Two of them went into the grocery store. The other one was Virgil! As soon as his feet hit the ground, he started to run, never bothering to dodge the puddles.

That's when I noticed that he was wearing a backpack. Maybe he had a crow in it! I followed him home to find out. If he started building a coop, that meant he was guilty.

Virgil ran along the highway that led into town. He turned onto a gravel driveway. He came to a place where there were several house trailers. At one of those, he stopped and jumped over three steps onto the porch. He disappeared inside.

I sat on the porch roof and waited. I cocked my head and listened for cawing from inside his home. Not a sound. For a long while I stayed, but Virgil did not come out.

Just as I was about to give up and fly off, a black car pulled up and parked in front of Virgil's home. The car door opened and a man stepped out. He was a tall, strong-looking man with hair as black as crow feathers—just like Virgil's. He wore high, black leather boots. His heels clicked on the pavement as he walked toward Virgil's home. I heard him knock on the door. He went inside.

I wondered if that man might be Virgil's daddy. Was he coming to say he was sorry for what he had done to Virgil and his mama? Or was he coming to hurt them again? Did Virgil know he was coming? Is that why he was running home? I decided to hang around a while longer.

Shortly, the stranger came out of the house. There was a woman with him. He had her by the hand. Her heels and his boots clicked on the sidewalk as they went to his car. He opened the door and she got in.

Just before he shut the door, a breeze blew her hair back from her face. I saw a scar by her eye and on her cheek. I knew that she must be Virgil's mama! What was the stranger going to do with her? And where was Virgil? He said his mama never goes anywhere alone. Why weren't Virgil or his granddaddy with her now?

I felt worried about her. And about Virgil, too. I waited until almost dark, but the stranger did not return Virgil's mama. Virgil did not come outside and build a coop.

I didn't feel safe alone in town at night, so I went home and roosted with my own flock. But I didn't rest easy.

At daylight, I hurried back to Virgil's. No school busses in sight. If Virgil is in trouble, there won't be a bus driver to save him this time.

I landed on his porch roof. No sign of the black car. No sound from inside the house. Just after sunrise, I saw the stranger's car coming up the gravel drive.

I cawed my danger warning five times. No use. There was no response. The car parked in front of the house trailer. The high-booted man got out of his car. Virgil's mama wasn't with him.

His fist was wrapped around something dark, and he hid that hand in his jacket pocket. Was it a weapon? I couldn't see.

With clicking strides he hurried up to the steps and onto the porch. I heard the door open and shut. I made up my mind that if he came out with Virgil, I would dive bomb him, as my Maw had done to Smokey.

How long did I wait? No way to tell. Waits always seem interminable—especially when I'm on high alert.

At last, I heard the door open and someone moving on the porch. It was Virgil! He jumped over the front steps and hit the pavement running. He wasn't wearing a jacket or his baseball cap.

I flew after him. His feet kicked up gravel as he tore down the driveway. He turned right and ran along the side of the highway. I thought he was headed for the grocery market to ask for help. But no.

Virgil barreled past the store's parking lot and continued down the berm, past a number of houses. I flew along, high enough to be safely above the fast moving cars and trucks.

If Virgil was in danger, why didn't he go to a house? Or flag down a car to get help? Virgil might be in a different kind of trouble. What if he had killed his daddy with that birthday knife?

Virgil finally stopped running. He looked both ways before bolting across the highway. From the other side, he continued uphill on a country road for a short distance.

At the next intersection, he turned right again and ran along a road that paralleled a pasture stream. It was all uphill from there.

Now I knew where he was going! He was headed for Kevin's house. But why?

Magic

I could have beaten Virgil by flying over the hill. But I thought I should keep an eye on him, in case the black car drove up, and the stranger tried to grab him.

As we approached our destination, I could see Kevin way back by the shed, chopping wood. He looked up and saw Virgil nearing his house.

Kevin stopped chopping and yelled, "Hey, Virgil! I tried to call you. This dead tree fell across the stream and Daddy cut it up. Daddy will pay us to split this up for fi…"

Virgil had gotten close enough for Kevin to see that something wasn't right. Virgil's hair and shirt were soaked with sweat, and his face was red. He began to stagger. Kevin dropped his ax and ran to meet him.

He put his hands on Virgil's shoulders to steady him and said, "What's goin' on?"

"My mama…" Virgil was out of breath. He gasped for air. He could barely talk. He bent over at the waist and put his hands on his knees. "Mama…got…." Virgil's sides heaved.

Kevin looked alarmed. "Is she OK? Tell me what happened!"

Virgil, still panting heavily, nodded. "She… got a… kitten." He began coughing.

One side of Kevin's mouth drew up and he squinted at Virgil. "Virgil. I know you ain't run four miles to tell me your mama got a kitten! You're dehydrated. Here." Kevin grabbed a chunk of the tree trunk and set it on end to make a stool. "Set yourself down and catch your breath. I'll fetch some water."

Kevin dashed to the house and came back in a flash with two water bottles. Virgil twisted the cap off one, leaned forward, and poured half the water over his already wet head. He smeared some over his face. Then he tipped up the bottle and drank the rest. He opened the second bottle and drank it dry.

Kevin dragged over another chunk of wood. He stood with one foot on it, arms across his knee, waiting for Virgil to regain his composure. "You OK now?"

"Yeah. Thanks, man. I just couldn't wait to tell you."

"OK. What's this about a kitten?"

"Back in July, a little fluffy white kitten with pink paws and blue eyes started hangin' around our trailer. Mama brought it inside, and she was cuddling it and strokin' it. Ya' know. And she asked Pap could she keep it.

"Pap set straight up in his recliner chair and said, 'Hell yes! That cat is magic!' So Mama asked what did he mean. He said, 'Honey, it's made a smile appear on your face that I ain't seen for years.'"

"So Mama named that kitten Magic. She made an appointment with that new vet to git shots an' all.

"Yeah. Dr. Duran. My sister took her dog to him."

"Right. Duran. Mateo Duran. And I went into the office with her, 'cause Mama's so shy, and she don't like to talk. But Dr. Duran kept askin' her questions—the kind you can't answer by just shakin' your head. When I tried to answer for her, he held his finger up to shush me, and kept lookin' at her. Like he was waitin' for her to talk.

"I could tell he was doin' it on purpose. And it worked. Mama was talkin' but she kept lookin' at Magic. The doctor kept lookin' at Mama. Kindly like.

"After he finished the exam and the shots, he picked up the kitten and talked to it face-to-face—like it was a Person. He said, 'Listen to me, Magic. You are a very lucky kitten. You have found a lovely, kind, and generous lady to adopt you. So you be a good kitty, and don't give her any trouble.'

"He gave Mama medicine for the cat and made an appointment to come back for more shots and to git her spayed. When all was done, he walked us to the door and held it open for Mama. He said it was a pleasure meeting us.

"A couple weeks later, we was in Cox's store—Pap and Mama and me. We was in the pet food aisle. And there was Dr. Duran. He was gittin' dog food. He come over and said hey and introduced hisself to Pap.

"Well, Pap was wearin' his Marine veteran cap. And the doctor noticed that and smiled. He said, 'Once a Marine, always a Marine!' He said he's a retired Marine. Then the two of them was all 'Oorah' and talkin' Marine stuff. You know.

"So Dr. Duran was sayin' that he grew up on his family's ranch in Texas. I guess that's why he wears them cowboy boots. He enlisted right out of school. He was an MP. After four years, he got to be a K-9 handler. He trained them Belgian Malinois dogs. That's the kind he has now. Her name is Ally.

"Anyways, then he went into the reserves. He said he had a buddy in the service who was from southwest Virginia. He said the guy was always braggin' on this area and sayin' what a special place this is. Duran wanted to study to become a veterinarian, so he decided to apply to Virginia Tech. They got a veterinary program.

"He said he done his internship right here with Dr. Alexander when she was just about to retire. He bought out her practice. Then he bought a big farm for his four horses.

"So Pap invited him to come over for a beer and to talk about the corps. He said he'd do that. And he did. And he brought flowers. And Mama cooked us all a real nice supper.

"And he brought his guitar and asked could he play some tunes for us. Well, sure! He plays real good. He sang some real funny songs, and Mama was laughin'. Made Pap and me feel good to hear Mama laugh like that.

"Then he invited us to go to Roanoke with him. And we all went to the art museum, and the Virginia Museum of Transportation and the O. Winston Link Museum."

"Awesome! Winston Link was a genius photographer!"

"Yeah! Amazing! We had a great time! We all ate supper at a really nice Thai restaurant over there."

"Well, later, he asked Mama if she'd care to go out with him. Her and him have been dating for months now. He's been takin' us to his place sometimes on Sundees and teachin' us both to ride. Mama's real good at it, too.

"Kevin, Dr. Duran treats my mama wonderful. Like she deserves."

"He sounds like a good man, Virgil."

"Well, here's the thing now. Last evenin' he took her to a contradance and then out to supper. She said he told her he loved her and would she marry him. She said yes."

"Oh, wow!"

"Yeah! But that ain't all of it. He said he wanted to ask Pap's permission. So after breakfast this mornin' he come over and asked Pap. Of course, he agreed. Then he asked me if it was acceptable to me!

"And then Dr. Duran got down on one knee and proposed to Mama. He pulled a box out of his pocket, and there was a engagement ring for her. Man, it was like somethin' out of a movie!"

Kevin was smiling a wide smile. He said, "Virgil, that is awesome! I'm so happy for y'all."

"They're gettin' married over Christmas break. But first, we're all flyin' out to Texas for Thanksgiving to meet his family. He said they can't wait to meet us."

"Hey great! And you're going to get that jet ride you were wishing for."

Virgil stood and put his hands on Kevin's shoulders. "You understand what this means, don't ya'? It means my mama is safe. She's safe!"

The boys gave each other a big hug. Then Kevin said, "I gotta' hand it to you, Virgil. When you tell a story, you start at the beginning." He gave Virgil a punch in the shoulder.

Virgil laughed. "Where else?"

"Let's go inside and get some ham sandwiches. And some of Mama's banana pudding."

"Sounds great!" Virgil looked back at the giant pile of wood behind them. "Then I'll help ya' with that, Kevin. Oughta make a cord or more. We can split that up in no time this afternoon."

Belonging

Tell Me About Daddy

One day I watched Ashley in the woods as she set out peanuts, pieces of apples, and piles of grain in one of her feeding spots on Charry Ridge. I was very interested in those peanuts.

Katelyn came trudging up the path with her tongue hanging out. She was bent forward and her arms dangled from her shoulders. "Uuuh! That was a long climb! And I'm sooo hot! I'm all out of breath and about to di-eee." She stood up straight.

"If you were all out of breath, you would wouldn't be talkin' so much and doin' all that dramatic actin'. My water canteen's right there, if you want it."

"I do! Thanks!" Katelyn took a long drink. She looked at her sister for a moment and said, "Ashley, will you help me with my homework?"

"Math again?"

"No. I'm doin' good in that now. But my teacher has us doin' this assignment called Roots and Wings. We're supposed to learn about our ancestors. You and Granny are the only ancestors I have."

Ashley chuckled. "Sweetie, I am not your ancestor. You could say I'm your sibling, but I ain't nobody's ancestor."

"Oh, yeah. Well, you know what I mean."

"Okay. How can I be of service to you, younger sibling?" Ashley took the canteen from Katelyn and drank.

Katelyn tilted her head slightly and said, "Ashley, tell me about Daddy."

"Why? "

"'Cause you can remember and I can't. You don't never say nothin' about him, and Granny just talks about when he was a boy. I want to know about him when he was our daddy."

Ashley turned her back to Katelyn and was silent. She walked a short distance, stopped, and pressed her shoulder against the furrowed bark of a tulip poplar. Her head drooped forward.

Katelyn stiffened both arms by her sides, doubled her fists and stomped her foot. "Ashley Belle Morgan, it ain't fair! It's like I ain't got no roots at all. It's like you had a daddy and I didn't!"

Ashley whirled around. Her fierce eyes were red, and her cheeks and chin dripped tears. "Well, if you never had a daddy, you never lost him. I did! And if you never had a daddy, you never miss him. I do!"

Ashley's lips trembled. She covered her face with her hands and sobbed.

Katelyn drew back her head, and her blue eyes widened. She rushed to Ashley and embraced her. Ashley rested her forehead on her sister's.

Rubbing Ashley's back, Katelyn pleaded, "Oh, Sissy, don't cry. Please. I never seen you cry before. I'm sorry. I'm so sorry. Please don't cry no more. I won't never ask nothin' about him again."

Ashley drew a deep breath and let it come slowly out her mouth. Backing away, she looked directly into her sister's face. Barely above a whisper, she said, "No. No, Katelyn. You're right. You and I had a daddy. He loved us both, and he would want you to know about him. So do I."

She brushed her cheeks with the backs of her hands. "It's just hard for me to talk…because I miss him so much." Her dark eyes grew moist again. "But I will. Come up here with me tomorrow morning, and I will share something with you."

Ashley gathered all her drawing materials. She stuffed them and the canteen into her backpack, and slung it over her shoulder. "Let's go home now."

Katelyn nodded. The two girls held hands and walked down the path toward home without saying another word.

The Letter

At the same place the next morning, I waited for the girls. They came together after sunup and sat side-by-side on a low, wide rock.

"I've been keeping something since the day Daddy sent me here, Katelyn." Ashley opened her backpack and took out an envelope. "I've been hiding this letter in the lining of my backpack. It's my most precious possession, so I always keep it close to me. Daddy gave it to me the last time I saw him. He said not to open it until you asked about him. I never wanted that day to come."

"But why, Ashley?"

"Because when I open it, it will be final. His words in this letter are the last words from our daddy. There will never be anything more. I know it seems silly, but I just feel that once I read this letter, that will really be the end."

Katelyn rested her head on Ashley's shoulder and said, "I see. You don't have to read it now, if you don't want to yet."

"That's very kind, Katelyn. But you did ask. So it's time." Ashley tore open the envelope with her pencil. Her hands trembled. She unfolded a thick set of pages and read.

Dearest Ashley Belle and Katelyn,

The most important thing for you to know is that you both were loved by your mama and me before you were born and every minute since. Each of you is wanted and loved.

I'd give anything to be able to stay in this world and be with you as you are growing up. But that's just not going to be possible. So it comforts me to know that the people I love most are all together.

Ashley, you have may have some memories of us. But, Katelyn, you were too little to recall anything about me or your mama. This letter is the only way I have to share with you things about my life and about hers.

I want this letter to be read when Katelyn is old enough to ask questions and understand some explanations about why you girls lived with your granny instead of your parents.

Your Granny Alma was a wonderful mama to me. She gave me all the care, support, inspiration, and guidance a child could ever want. I know she will do the same for you.

I grew up without my own daddy. I was blessed to be raised on the Morgan family farm by my mama and my Papaw, Spencer Cleve Morgan. He taught me how to do farm work, helped me with Scout projects, taught me how to flatfoot dance, how to shave, how to drive a car, and how to fix one.

When I turned fourteen, Papaw took me to tour the Norfolk Naval Station. I was enthralled by the ocean and the Navy ships. After that, I thought of nothing else but joining the Navy.

The summer before my senior year in high school, I went to the Old Fiddlers' Convention in Galax with my mama. There, I met a girl named Pamela Katsaros, from West Virginia. She was the best flatfoot dancer I'd ever seen. As I got to know her better, I realized that she was also smart, funny, and tenderhearted. After I met Pamela, I thought of nothing else but marrying her and joining the Navy.

Your mama was a cheerleader. Because she was petite, she was the flier—the one that gets tossed up in the air by the other cheerleaders. She had the talent and self-confidence to do that!

We talked on the phone and wrote letters to each other. Whenever we could, we went out together—to dances, or to a movie and a meal at the mall.

We had a lot in common. We both were good students, liked the same kinds of music, sports, and books. Neither of us had siblings, and we both were eager to have a family of our own.

She knew I had my heart set on being a seaman, and she was fine with that. She liked the idea of living near the coast. Her dream was to be a full-time homemaker and mother.

Growing up, she hadn't gotten much time with her own parents. Her daddy drove truck and was gone a lot. Her mama worked in a biscuit shop. So she was often left with her granny or her daddy's sister, Nelda.

Right after we graduated we got married. I enlisted in the Navy. Life could not have been better. I had married the love of my life, I enjoyed my career, and your mama and I got along great. In everything we did, we were partners. Never had a cross word between us.

Your mama could do anything she put her mind to. She was resourceful and creative. She sewed your clothes, and most of her own. She made our simple little quarters on the base a comfortable and inviting place to come home to. She was a great cook, an avid reader, and a whiz at playing Trivial Pursuit.

Ashley, here's a story about how we chose your name. Your mama said that her Aunt Nelda had a collection of Ashley Belle porcelain dolls in her china cabinet. Nelda would save up her money all year, so she could travel to Hillsville for the Labor Day weekend flea market. Every year, she'd get herself another doll there.

When your mama was little she'd beg to play with those dolls. Aunt Nelda would tell her, "No, child! Them's not toys. Them's collectables. Someday them dolls will be worth a fortune!"

So when your mama saw our first beautiful baby girl, she said, "Now, I got my own Ashley Belle!"

Katelyn, your name has a story, too. Your mama and I were fans of the great West Virginia journalist and singer-songwriter Kate Long. So you were named for her. We also wanted to name you in honor of my mama, Alma Lyn. We thought of giving you two names, but decided to combine them into Katelyn.

Of course, everyone who saw you girls noticed that Ashley was blond like her daddy, with big dark eyes like her mama's. And Katelyn got my blue eyes and her mama's black curly hair.

Just a month after you were born, Katelyn, I was diagnosed with juvenile ALS. There is no cure. I was medically discharged from the Navy. We moved to West Virginia, closer to your mama's family and her old friends.

We'd had a happy life up until then. My illness hit us hard. I think your mama was grieving for me, even before I was gone. She was trying to cope with a painful reality. Neither of us had ever used drugs of any kind. She was probably depressed and had no idea what kind of trap she was falling into.

One morning in late November that year, I found a note from your mama. In it, she said she was sorry, said she would always love us, but she had to go away. She said not to look for her, because she was no good any more. She hoped we would forgive her someday, but she'd never forgive herself.

The phone rang, and it was your Granny Jean. She said your mama had been over there and acting strangely. The Percocet pills for her arthritis pain were missing after your mama had left. I checked our medicine cabinet, and my prescription for depression medicine was also missing.

Your mama got some money at an ATM. Not a lot. She disappeared. All of us searched. All her friends and family and the police. None of us was ever able to find her.

I hope that by the time you read this, she will have come back to you. Some people can become addicted very easily to the medicines that were prescribed for me. More such cases are being reported all the time. I have found that meditation—not medication—has helped me to handle what I've been dealing with.

No one goes through this life without making mistakes. Your mama's mistake cost her so much. I hope you girls hold no bitterness toward her. She did truly love us all and never meant anyone any harm.

Ashley was in first grade at that time, and she could do a lot for herself. But I knew I didn't have the strength or energy to take care of an infant. So your Granny Alma took you, Katelyn, to stay with her. It hurt so to give you up, but I knew I was putting you into the most loving care.

My health got worse over the next few years. Finally, it was time for me to go into nursing care at the Virginia Veterans Care Center in Roanoke.

That's when Ashley went to stay with Granny and you at the farm, Katelyn. I had prepared this letter and entrusted it to Ashley to keep until you were ready for it.

Being around old-time musicians, you will surely hear a Carter Family song that asks "Will the circle be unbroken by and by?" I don't know if I will meet my daddy for the first time, or see Papaw again in the sky. And I'm not going to promise you that I will be up in heaven watching over you for the rest of your lives. If I can, I surely will, but what comes next is all a mystery to me.

I have come to believe the circle won't need to be repaired, because it can never can be broken. We are all part of an eternal cycle.

Confronting my own death now feels in some way familiar—like seeing the ocean that first time. I'm facing something so incomprehensibly profound, so overwhelmingly powerful and mysterious I can only stand in wonder before it. Death seems as miraculous as birth.

All I can hope to leave with you is the knowledge that you have always been loved. That is the most important thing there is. I can only tell you that being your daddy is the greatest joy of my life, and I am so grateful for you both.

Your loving daddy

"And life is eternal and love is immortal, And death is only a horizon, And a horizon is nothing more, Than the limit of our sight."— Quaker Prayer

When Ashley finished reading, she folded the pages and sat gazing at them. Both girls were silent for a while. Then Katelyn spoke.

"See, Ashley," she said, "It ain't the end."

"It never will be." Ashley smiled.

And that's when I knew I was ready to face the Ocean.

The First Assemblage

I talked to Maw about the letter and what Scott Morgan said about the Ocean. I told her that Ashley had been afraid to read the letter, but after she did she felt better. Maybe I will feel better about the Ocean after I meet it. Maw said that when the long nights come, we would fly together to the great roost near the beach.

I thought about Katelyn's longing to know of things she cannot remember. I thought there must be many things I cannot remember. The world did not begin the day I hatched. I wanted to know more about the days before me.

The oldest being I know, the one who can remember longer than anyone, is Owenasa. I settled among her soft-needled branches and spoke.

"Owenasa, you are the eldest tree on this mountain, aren't you?"

"I am."

"So you remember the long past. I want to know what you can remember."

"Much has changed since I was a sprout. Those were the days of the First Assemblage. Chestnut trees were abundant here. They fed many creatures. But now they are all gone.

Also fragrant hemlock trees lived here. Now most of them are gone, too.

"The forest was home to bison, elk, mountain lions, and wolves. You have never met any of them. They're gone from here now. Beaver, mink, turkey, opossum, bobcat, and fox were abundant, but now they are few. Great golden clouds of Monarch butterflies used to pass through. Now they are not so many.

"The First Assemblage included the Peoples. They were human beings who lived throughout the mountain forests when there was much food for them. They lived in small tribes, not too many together. When they traveled, they usually walked. So they were called by other forest creatures Peoples Who Walk on the Earth.

"Their homes were of wood and animal skins. Their food was plants and meat from animals they hunted or caught. They made clothes from animal skins and plant fibers. Their medicine was from plants. Their tools from stone and shells, wood and clay, bone and horn.

"They created art from feathers, bone, shells, clay, and wood. All that the Peoples had, they received from the life of the forest. They took only what they needed, not too much.

"Forest life was balanced. The Peoples respected the balance. Their ways did not disturb it.

"But the Peoples often made war upon one another. Wars caused much wounding and grief. A great teacher came to the Peoples north of here to remedy this. His name was Deganawida. His message was that the nations of Peoples should come together as one great confederacy and live in peace with one another.

"Deganawida planted a white pine he called the Great Tree of Peace. That pine was one of my ancestors. Deganawida told five nations of Peoples in the north to join into one confederacy, as five needles of the White Pine are held together in one cluster.

"He said that the roots of the White Pine point in the four directions. Other nations from every direction may find their way into the confederacy to shelter in the Great Tree of Peace.

"For a very long time, peace within the confederacy lasted, and the five nations grew strong in it. One more nation joined, but many did not. Those continued their wars and grew weaker.

"Here, in these mountains where you live now, once the Cherokee People and the Tutelo People lived during hunting seasons. Like many others of the First Assemblage, they are gone or rare. Those who remain in these mountains, cannot live in the ways that their Peoples once lived when the forest was balanced.

"By the time your ancestors arrived here, I was a tall, strong young tree. The crows chose me as their place on Charry Ridge. They had lived among Peoples who spoke Cherokee, and they called me by a word from that language. They called me Owenasa—Home."

The Second Assemblage

"The Second Assemblage included other humans. They came on wheels. At first only wagons drawn by mules, oxen, or horses. The ways of those humans were different from the Peoples who had always been here. They wanted to be self-sufficient individuals. They wanted independence. So they were known in the forest as Persons. We call them Persons Who Roll on the Earth.

"For a time, they kept the balance of the forest. Later, they yielded to the Empires. The Empires were far away, but they wanted all the riches the mountains had to offer.

"The Empires wanted the fur of animals and feathers of birds. They took too many, and the numbers of those creatures became fewer and fewer. Also, they took the gold and colorful stones the mountains had held for ages. They coveted the trees of the forest. The Persons offered up all these things, until the mountains were nearly naked and the land was impoverished.

"Next, the Empires wanted things long dead and buried deep within the mountains. The Persons dug death from beneath the mountains and fed it to their machines. They heated their homes and made their clothing and medicine and food from the death they harvested.

"The Empires wanted gashes cut into the mountains to make roads and rails to roll upon. The Persons cut them. When the Empires called for war, Persons sacrificed their sons and daughters, that the Empires may take possession of Persons in other lands."

I was confused. "What are the Empires? How can I recognize one if I see it? Why do they have so much power?" I asked Owenasa.

"You will not see an Empire. They are nobody. They have no body. They exist only in the imagination of Persons.

"Because they have no appearance, they are represented by symbols. Persons wear the symbols of Empires on their clothing, their rolling vehicles, and every item they possess. They believe what the Empires say, eat and drink what the Empires allow, and wear what the Empires permit.

"The Persons bestow the Empires with all the power that is their own. Persons work for the Empires, not for themselves. They sacrifice their time, labor, skill, creativity, and health for the sake of these Empires, which are ever hungry for more. The Empires are given rights and privileges greater than those any Person may have.

"The Empires poison the land, the water, and the sky. And so the Persons become poisoned themselves. All that they use and consume is made from the death they dig up. None of it can return to life, and none of it can die. It can only be discarded."

"Owenasa, what will become of the world with these Empires in charge?" I asked.

"I can tell you only what I remember and observe. I cannot foresee the future, Dear One."

"Then can you tell me why the Persons do these things?"

"I do not understand. Perhaps they do not understand."

Wings

The next afternoon, I perched on the rail fence by the Morgan sisters' house. Katelyn was outside on the front porch. She yelled, "Aaash-leee! Come out here and help me. Granny wants us to transplant these daffodil bulbs to over there by the gate.

Ashley stepped out and said, "Great! Those will be real pretty next spring. Let's go." The screen door banged shut behind her as she hurried down the porch steps and into the shed.

Katelyn carried a cardboard box of bulbs, and Ashley followed with a rake and spade. At the gate, Ashley dug along the fence line. Both girls began setting bulbs into the soil.

Katelyn stopped for a moment and gazed into the sky. "Asp-uh-ray-shuns. I think that is a very pleasant word. Don't you?"

"It's lovely. Did you just learn it?"

"Yeah. It's from the Wings part of our Roots and Wings project at school. I told you about that."

"I remember," Ashley said as she patted soil over a cluster of bulbs.

"My teacher says our aspirations are the wings that will carry us up in life. We're havin' to write a report about our aspirations."

"That sounds like fun. So, what are your 'asp-uh-ray-shuns'?"

"Well, I will write about that I want to be a writer."

"What kind of writer do you aspire to be? A journalist? A novelist? A playwright?"

"No. Not that. I want to write stories for children like Beatrix Potter did. I'll make up stories about animals—like cows, pigs, fireflies, chickens, blue jays, dogs, ducks, frogs, worms, mice, butterflies, bats, squirrels…"

"I get the idea," Ashley interrupted. "I remember how much you loved for me to read Peter Rabbit stories to you when you were little. And Dr. Seuss books. You liked those stories a lot, too."

"Yes! Especially *The Lorax*! But, that's not my only aspirations. I also want to write poems and songs. And I want to play old-time music at the fiddlers' convention like Granny does. And maybe someday, a long, long, loooong time in the future, my songs will be old-time music."

"Well, you have some grand aspirations, Katelyn. Are you going to read your report to me when it's finished?"

"Sure. Before I hand it in to Miss Palmer, you can check if my English is proper."

Ashley raised an eyebrow. "What do you mean 'proper'?"

"Well, I get my best grades in Language Arts. I always do good on my homework and tests. But when I'm tryin' to tell Miss Palmer something, she interrupts me and says to talk properly. I hate when she does that! I wish she would just listen to what I'm sayin' and not be tryin' to fix how I'm sayin' it."

"You know, Katelyn, Miss Palmer hasn't lived here long. Maybe she hasn't learned yet that there's lots of 'proper' ways to talk. There's nothing improper about the way mountain folks talk. Miss Palmer means for you to use something called 'Standard English.'

"It might be good for you to learn that kind of English in school. But when you're writing compositions from your heart, and when you talk to folks around here, you'd be right to keep your own language. It's just like old-time music. It's our heritage. Passed down through generations. It's somethin' to treasure."

"I see." Katelyn put the last of the bulbs into the soil. "Ashley, I guess your aspiration is to be an artist. Right?"

"Not really."

"Then how come you're always drawing everything you see? You draw your classmates, animals, flowers, leaves. You even draw mushrooms!"

"I like to draw." Ashley shrugged. "And by the way, your friend Beatrix Potter also drew mushrooms. She was a mycologist as well as a children's author."

"What's a mike-ologist?"

"A scientist who studies fungi. I read a library book about Potter's life. Anyway, drawing is one way I record my observations.

I also write notes about a lot of the things I observe in the woods.

"What kind of observations?"

"When I see a certain kind of animal, I mark what it's doing. Like if it's eating and what kind of food. Or if it's making a nest, or feeding its babies. I write down what I see plants doing—if they are making leaf buds, or blossoming, or dropping seeds. I write down whatever I see. I aspire to be a scientist and a conservationist—sort of like Jane Goodall."

"Who's she?"

"She studied chimpanzees in the Gombe forest in Tanzania. She didn't shoot them with tranquilizers or put them in laboratories. She just went to their home, sat with them, and listened and watched. That's how she learned everything."

"How did you know that?"

"I read about her in one of great granddaddy Spencer's old *National Geographic* magazines. Then I got one of her books from the library. She was able to demonstrate that the animals she studied are intelligent, have feelings, and can communicate with each other."

Katelyn shrugged. "Well, ever body knows that."

"But most scientists didn't believe it until Jane Goodall proved it."

Katelyn tilted her head. "So, are you going to live in the jungle in Africa when you grow up?"

"I'm hopin' I can be a conservationist right here. I want to study the wild animals and plants that live in the Blue Ridge Mountains. These are some of the most magnificent creatures in the world, and I want to understand them. I think I learn best with what I call the I.O.U. method."

"What's that?"

"Inquire. Observe. Understand. I believe all creatures are intelligent and communicate with each other in a language without words. People just don't realize yet how intelligent animals really are."

Katelyn stood up and brushed her dirty hands on the seat of her overalls. "Ashley, I think people just don't realize yet how intelligent you really are."

Nutcracker Sweet

I decided to go to the Parkway to contemplate fear, and the limit of my sight, and the mysterious Ocean. By the time I arrived there, I was feeling a bit peckish. I found some nuts under a hickory tree, but the shells were too hard to split with my beak. To crack the nuts, I decided to drop them from a high branch onto a pretty black and orange stone below.

I dropped a nut, and it hit the target. But it bounced off. I went down to check it. Nope. It hadn't cracked. So I took it back up and tried again. Bombs away!

Clunk. The nut struck again. I heard a muffled voice from below call out, "Ow! Dang! Cut that out, will ya'?" The voice seemed to be coming right out of the stone.

I flew down and landed beside it. I cocked my head and listened. Not a sound. "Hello?"

Slowly a head with a beak emerged from the stone. It blinked its two red eyes.

"Oh, wonderful!" I said. "You must be one of those ancient rocks that can speak about life when the Ocean was here! Please tell me the story."

Instead of answering me, the stone asked, "Has a nut hit you on your head?"

"No. Why?"

"Because you seem confused. You think you are speaking to a talking rock. I'm an Eastern Box Turtle—at least that's what Persons call me. And what in the world is an Ocean?"

"Oops. Sorry. My bad. I hope I didn't hurt you."

"Not injured. Just annoyed, but I'm fine."

"Good. Well, the Ocean, you see, is a place of vast water. Bigger than any pond around here. It used to be here, but it's far away now. I plan to go meet it."

"Interesting. Well, I was just on my way to some water, too. Not so far away. But I'm having a terrible morning."

"What's the problem?"

"Early today, I was on the other side of the road, searching in the high, dewy grass for slugs and worms to eat. The sun was getting warmer and the ground was beginning to dry. I was afraid the grass cutters might come. I'd never be able to outrun them, and they'd chop me to bits.

"You have legs?"

"Oh, yeah. See?" Box Turtle stretched out four legs. Two in the front and two in the back. The front feet had five toes with claws. The larger back feet had only four toes. He had a pointy little tail in back, too.

"Are you still hiding from the grass cutters under this stone?"

Box Turtle blinked. "I'm not under a stone. It's my shell. It's my home. I live in here."

"Want to come outside now?"

"I can't come outside. My home is part of my body. It goes wherever I go."

I could not imagine having to go through life with my nest on my back. But I didn't say that. Instead, I said, "It's a lovely home you have. Beautifully decorated."

"Thanks. So, as I was saying, I was trying to cross the road to the picnic area to look for food scraps. I was almost to the berm when a kid saw me. He ran over, picked me up, and started looking me over.

"That was scary. I was afraid he'd decide to take me home and make a pet of me. I don't want to leave here. If he had kidnapped me, I would have spent the rest of my life trying to find my way back to my territory."

"Oh, I understand. A boy captured me when I was a chick and tried to make me a pet. It was awful! How did you get away from your captor? Did you bite him?

"No. I wouldn't do that. I pulled my head, legs and tail inside and closed my shell. I pretended I wasn't at home. I didn't really escape. A woman called the boy. Instead of putting me down in the grass, he set me on my back in the middle of the road.

"He stood there for a few moments watching me struggle to turn over and get onto my feet. He was laughing. Then a man yelled at him and told him to quit playing in the road. He ran away.

"I was completely helpless. I could not turn over. If I'd stayed out there long enough, either a roller would've smashed me flat, or the heat of the sun would have cooked me. I thought I was doomed.

"But some hikers came out of the forest just in time. One of the women saw me and came over. She picked me up and carried me back to the grass on the side of the road I was trying to leave.

"She was just trying to help. At least I was right side up, but I had to start all over again. As I tried to cross the road the second time, a big roller came zooming along. Those are the worst killers of all! It was rolling much faster than is allowed on the Parkway.

"I'm slow. I knew I couldn't outrun it, so I tucked into my shell again and hoped it wouldn't crush me.

"The roller swerved and missed me, but the gust it created spun me about. Then I was facing the wrong way again and had to turn around.

"I was hot, tired, and desperate to get into some shade. Luckily, I managed to make it to this hickory tree to cool off in the moist leaf litter around the roots. I was having a nice nap when you started bombarding me.

"Oh, dear. You have had a troubled morning."

"Life for a Box Turtle is a series of near misses. The eggs in our mud nests are vulnerable to snakes, raccoons, and foxes in the spring. Lots of animals feast on us after we hatch, when we're still soft little babies.

"Slowly our shells grow strong and hard. Once we have those, we're pretty safe, and some of us live to a ripe old age. But Persons are always a problem for us."

I escorted my new friend to a small creek that was his desired destination. It was a long walk. He really is slow. He wished me good luck finding the Ocean. I bid him farewell and long life.

He was glad to slip back into the refreshing water. I was glad to return to the soul-soothing sky.

As the Crow Flies

Gradually, the days had shortened. Perhaps, I thought, the sun is growing old and tired and needs more rest. Each dark, dangerous night was a bit longer than the one before. Now, Maw told me, it was time to begin our journey to the roost by the Ocean.

"We will fly in the direction of the sunrise for days to reach the crossroads where our roost meets at a place called Virginia Beach. We will travel as far as we can each day.

"At night we will roost with other flocks along the way. Some of those crows will join the trip, until many of us will be traveling together. There is safety in murders.

"Always we will roost at night in towns and cities, not in the forests or countrysides."

"Why, Maw?"

"Because we will be in unfamiliar territories. We won't know where predators may be lurking. Cities are brightly lit at night. So it's easier to spot trouble and to find safe places to escape."

"Ah! Of course."

"I know of many roadside parks and restaurants along the way, where we can pick up a bite to eat. You will not go hungry. Stay close to me. Watch and learn, Darling One."

I understood our travel plan, but I was too excited to sleep well. As the first light seeped into the sky, before the drowsy sun had shone his face above the treetops, we took off.

We were both strong fliers, and we made good time each day. Often we traveled along roadways, keeping above the traffic. Once, Maw signaled to me to follow her to a landing. She lit inside an open truck full of garbage.

"It's a trick I learned at the last roost," she said. "We can cover a lot of ground while we rest and have a meal."

"I like it!" I said. "So much to scavenge here!"

"But don't overeat. If this truck turns in a direction we don't want to travel, we will fly back onto our route."

Maw was right about city lights. Cities are never dark. Back home, I had seen some lights at night. And I had seen the green-yellow-red light at the crossroad in the center of town. I knew that was a signal to tell the rollers when to stop or go.

Colored lights were everywhere in cities! Strings of lights stretched like clothes lines across the streets. Lights on poles brightened dark sidewalks and parking lots. Store windows were brightly lit. Red, green, yellow, and blue lights outlined roofs and fronts of houses. Colored lights glowed on trees in yards and on porches. Some lights blinked off and on. I wondered if that was some kind of signal too.

Of course, the lights weren't as wondrous as stars in the deep black nights back home, or fireflies in the meadow grasses, or flashes of lightning in a stormy sky, or sparkling colors in the morning dewdrops. Still, they were quite nice.

At one of the places we rested over night, I met some local juveniles. They hadn't been to Virginia Beach, but they said there were some interesting things to do in this town. They took me along for a very merry side trip.

Adeste!

"Jet, there's a really cool happening this evening. Some of us have been to it before. Want to come with us?"

"Sure! But, first I have to talk to Maw."

"What are you? A nestling? Scared of Maw?"

"No. Not scared. But she cares about me, and I don't want to cause her worry. She's been through a lot, you know."

"Well, hurry up! The bells are already ringing. Tell her we'll be right over there by that big oak with the dead leaves. By the white tower. See it?"

Maw said she knew about the event. She had been there once. She told me to go and have fun with my new friends. So off we went. The oak was near a large, white house with a tower on top. The bells we heard were inside that tower.

I had never seen windows like the ones in this house. They were not clear, so you couldn't see inside. Instead, the windows were made of several colors. Bright lights inside the house glowed through them. They reminded me of trees back home, when I had seen sunlight shining through colored leaves.

"Oh, very nice! Bell music and colorful windows. Thanks for bringing me," I said. I was about to leave.

"But, wait! There's more! Come to the other side of the building."

I followed them to a white pine just like Owenasa, but much younger and smaller. This really reminded me of home. Below us was a large gathering of Persons. Most were facing a small shed and singing songs I had never heard. I couldn't even understand the words: *Adeste Fideles, laeti triumphantes. Venite, venite in Bethlehem.*

Tied to the shed was a little donkey. Beside the shed were several men with long sticks and some sheep. On the other side of the shed were three men wearing golden hats. All the men had long beards. There were lots of little children in white dresses, wearing foil circles on their heads and phony wings on their backs.

"I never saw men wearing long dresses back home."

"They're just in disguise for this special event. Never mind about them. Look in the shed."

"I can't see."

"Come on down here and get a better view."

I dropped to a lower branch and looked. Inside the shed I could see another hairy-faced man in a dress. He was with a lady who had a scarf over her hair. Both were kneeling and holding their hands together, just as Kevin had when he was talking to Heavenly Father in the woods! I started to wonder if Heavenly Father had followed us here to keep an eye on me.

Between the man and woman there was a nest of straw with a baby in it! He wasn't holding his own hands. He seemed to be waving them at everybody.

"Why are the Persons doing this?" I asked.

"No idea. But they act like this whenever it's the season of long dark nights."

One of the little girls with fake wings walked over to the guys with the sheep, held out her arms, and shouted at them, "Fear not, for I bring you tidings of great joy. Unto you is born this day in the City of David…"

"Are we in the City of David?"

"No. They're just pretending. Shh."

Then I heard the little girl yell, "Peace on Earth. Good will to all men."

Hmm. Same symbol—a white pine. Same message—peace on earth.

"Oh!" I exclaimed. "That must be baby Deganawida!"

"Who? No, I don't think so. The Persons call this kid Jesus."

"Well, it was a great show. Very educational. Thanks for bringing me."

"If you like this, you should come back when the leaf buds begin to open again. These folks will hang Jesus on a cross, just like that one on top of the bell tower."

"No way! Why would they do that to a little baby?"

"Oh, by then he'll be a grown man."

I was amazed. "He must grow really fast!"

"For sure. It's miraculous! When he dies, there's blood. But don't worry. It's all fake. Well, better get back to the roost before dark. Race ya!"

I was just a bit disappointed, but I didn't mention it to the others. They would just say it was my own fault that I didn't get here soon enough to see the baby Person hatch. I've always wondered what color their egg shells are.

Anty Climax

After days of traveling east, we could smell salty air. Then we could see throngs of crows gathering like storm clouds in the trees. The noise of resounding caws, flapping wings, and roaring traffic on the highways was a bit overwhelming. We and our companions found some bare branches and settled into one of the trees.

"We're here at last!" Maw said. "What do you think?"

"It…it's awesome. Really, just…". I stopped and scratched myself. "Maw, actually, I don't feel so good. My wings are about worn out. I feel grimy, and I itch all over."

"Me too. Maybe we picked up more than a bite to eat in that last garbage truck. I'm really too tired to preen us both right now. I know what will make us feel better. Come on, let's go anting."

I had no idea what anting was, but I was ready to try anything.

Maw led me to a nearby park. She landed and walked around a bit, looking for something in the sand. "Over here they are! I'll show you what to do."

I joined her and watched as she picked up a few ants in her beak and rubbed them around in her feathers. "Try it," she said. "Press them hard between your feathers wherever you itch. Squeeze out the juice. It's good for your skin."

I grabbed a beakful and slathered the ant juice on myself. "Ahh! Oh, Maw, this is so refreshing!"

"Just what we needed after such a long journey."

We continued our anting and preening until we both felt clean and soothed.

Other crows landed nearby and began picking up ants. We didn't mind. There were plenty to go round.

An adult male was eyeing me. He walked over and said, "Hi, there. I couldn't help noticing that you're wearing a band. What study are you part of?"

No idea what he was talking about. "Sorry, I don't understand what you mean."

"Well, some of us are banded by researchers doing scientific studies of crows. I am part of a study being done at a university up north. See?" He turned and showed me a tag sticking out from his wing. It had marks like this: N8. I noticed that he also had bands on his leg. They were prettier than mine.

"When we are nestlings, researchers grab us out of trees on campus. They stick these tags on our wings to mark us, because to Persons, we all look alike. For some reason, they call me Nate. After they tag and band us, they put us back. Then they just watch everything we do."

I explained how I came to have my band.

"I'm thinking of moving south permanently. Better climate down here. Besides, I know the college students don't mean any harm, but I just don't like being watched all the time."

"I know just what you mean! Somebody called Heavenly Father is always watching me and the sparrow. It's unnerving. Are you by yourself?"

"This trip I am," he said sadly. "My mate died a couple of seasons ago, before we could finish building our nest. She was one of many crows who succumbed to the same illness. I heard some researchers and students on campus call it West Nile disease. It was fatal to every crow it infected."

"Very sorry for your loss." I said. Right away, I could imagine the possibilities. "I'm here with my Maw. I'd like to introduce you to her. She's also a widow."

"Love to meet her," he said.

I just knew that the two of them would make a good match. After introductions, Nate said he could go for some seafood. He invited us to come along. I wasn't ready to face the Ocean yet. I said I was more tired than hungry. I wanted to rest. So Maw and Nate went off together.

When Maw returned later, I said, "I had one main reason for coming to the roost. First thing in the morning, I want to do what I came to do."

"Very well," she said. "No use putting it off. Would you like me to come with you?"

"Thanks, but I think this is something I should do on my own."

"As you wish."

"I will leave early."

"Fly straight toward the light. You can't miss the Ocean."

Sea Change

Before sunrise, I settled on the damp shore. All was quiet. Little wet ruffles ran up close to me whispering "Sh, sh, sh." As I stood in awe before the vast water, the last stars dimmed. The sun slipped up between the edges of the sea and the sky. It lit a bright path between itself and me.

A soft voice spoke. It said, "You have returned. Welcome, Little Bird."

"But, I have not returned. I've never been here before."

"You have not been to the Ocean, but the Ocean has always been in you. Do you hear how your heart beats in rhythms like the waves? Do you feel how your breath ebbs and flows within you like the tides?

"Yes. I do."

"I embrace every land. To every place I send winds and nourishing rains. All that lives on land comes from the Ocean. All returns to me. Deep within my heart are many lives that never come ashore. They exist far beyond the limit of your sight."

"Do you mean that you created all of life?"

"I am not the Creator. I am the Essence. Without me, the world is a cinder."

"I live in the mountains. Is it true that you swallow up mountains?"

"Look out upon my face. Do you see the white-capped rows of blue that rise above the surface?"

"I see the waves are like the mountains called the Blue Ridge when they wear crests of snow."

"Do you see that those waves fall and return to me, and are reformed and rise again and again and again? The mountains are waves that move more slowly. They rise and fall and rise, as they must."

"So you don't really want to destroy the mountains?"

"I don't want anything. I have no desire. I obey the law, as I must. You see, Little Bird, the sun and moon, the stars and all that has form must obey, for the law holds the balance.

"Only the Empires violate the law. For the sake of the Empires, many Persons commit the impermissible."

"I have heard of the Empires. They steal the dead from under the mountains."

"Also they reach beneath my waters and suck out what has been long dead. From that they make materials that cannot live or die. Those return to me also. They come as fumes sprayed in the air, as filth spewed into the water, and as debris strewn on the land. All is carried back to me. It poisons the life within me. It contaminates the life on land and kills even the Persons who consume the materials."

"Why do the Persons submit to the Empires?"

"Many do not understand the law."

"Ocean, what will become of this world?"

"It will change. That is the law. Even the Empires will rise and fall."

"But how will it change?"

"I cannot foresee. My sight has limits, too."

The Ocean and I parted ways. I will return to it someday, in some way.

Back at the roost Maw asked, "Did you make peace with the Ocean, Dear One?"

"The Ocean made peace in me," I told her.

Roosting Habits of Persons

For generations some crows have been observing the behavioral patterns of Persons who congregate in large numbers at the beach. Each year crows share their observations and consider what they might mean to the crows and communities of animals who live in the area.

One of the local birds who was an authority on the subject began. "We have seen more and more Persons coming to the beach, and in warmer times of year, the increases are especially significant. Seagulls report that, by using the tags on the backs of rollers, they have tracked Persons leaving the area to destinations far inland. Their studies confirm that many Persons travel long distances to roost here briefly.

"Crows studying this seasonal roosting behavior have perched on hotel balconies and peered into windows of the individual compartments. They confirm that these spaces are temporary nesting sites for individuals or small groups. The Persons occupy these spaces for several days, move out, and are replaced by other Persons.

"Based on observations we hypothesize that the Persons beach themselves for various reasons. They may be seeking mates. They may be collecting here to eat seafood. Perhaps they are exchanging information about good places to breed and raise their young.

"Some still unanswered questions are:

- Do all Persons beach themselves?
- Do some do that once and never again?
- Do the same individuals come on multiple occasions ?
- Do some come and remain as permanent residents?
- Just how far do Persons travel to attend these gatherings at the beach?

"So those are the big questions regarding roosting behavior *per se.* However, we continue to study other fascinating behaviors."

A different old crow began to discuss that topic. "Clearly, beaching behaviors have something to do with molting, as Persons wear far less clothing at the beach than they tend to wear in most other locations. We also observe that they frequently spread a greasy substance on themselves or their mates and then lie about on the shore. This grooming behavior is likely an effort to rid themselves of parasites. Seabirds have reported that some ingredients in the greasy stuff are toxic to Ocean coral."

"Another puzzling behavior is that during beaching, Persons often sit under umbrellas. Umbrella use is normally observed during rainy weather. At the beach, however, umbrellas are frequently seen when it is not raining.

"We are also curious about the purpose of dark glasses. This may be a form of trickery, to keep others from seeing where the eyes of the Persons are directed, or it may be a form of display to attract potential mates."

"We also note that some Persons engage in repetitive behaviors that seem to have no purpose. For example, some will enter the water with a large board, stand upon the board, and allow a wave to carry them back to shore. They will do this over and over again. Another repetitive behavior is batting a ball back and forth across a net. These behaviors do not appear to be associated with food gathering, mating, caring for offspring, grooming, or other survival needs. Perhaps these activities are indications of boredom. However, some have suggested that these are examples of play behavior. As you know, play behaviors are demonstrated only by highly intelligent animals, such as crows."

Someone in the crowd cawed out, "If Persons are intelligent, why do they act so stupid?"

Another voice added, "Yeah! That's what you ought to be researching!" These remarks were met with jeers of Haw-Haw-Haw. When the commotion subsided, a final speaker talked about ambulatory behaviors.

"Persons are often observed to walk or run along the edge of the water, especially in early morning or evening. Although Persons possess the ability to walk on their hind legs, it is widely known that they prefer to float, ride, glide, slide, elevate, escalate, or skate whenever possible. The beach runners and walkers are not fleeing from anything, nor are they pursuing any prey or apparent destination. There are no opponents, so we know that these are not competitive races. The purpose of this curious behavior continues to baffle researchers."

Rebels With Caws

After the conference, I noticed a large flock of young crows in a nearby tree. They cawed and flapped excitedly. One young male was doing most of the talking. He was a handsome adolescent fellow. Still too young to mate, but the females already found him attractive. The male crows paid close attention to what he said. Most seemed to be in agreement.

The speaker was saying, "You all heard the discussion over there. Those old crows are just going to keep studying the problem. Meanwhile, we and our seabird friends are being killed. All because of the senseless and destructive ways of Persons. It's up to us, the young generation, to do something about it."

"Yeah! This is our roost," another male chimed in.

"And our Ocean and beach!" added a pelican who was listening.

"Look," the leader continued. "We've all tried. All of us creatures have tried to adapt to living with Persons. Where has it gotten us? Granted, some Persons are trying to help us, but this is our fight. If we're going to have any chance to survive in this world with them, they have got to be the ones to change. Not us!"

"That's right!" a female responded. "We need to take this fight to them. For the sake of our chicks."

"And in honor of our ancestors who thrived in this world before Persons unbalanced it," said another.

"And in memory of our friends and loved ones who've had their lives and habitat destroyed by these invaders!" I put in.

These comments were met with caws and wing pulsing.

"Who's with me then?" the leader asked the crowd.

"We are!" they cawed in reply.

"Wait a minute," said a single voice. "There won't be any violence, will there? I'm not into that."

The leader answered. "Violence is unnecessary and counter-productive. All we need to do is piss them off. Make being here so unpleasant, they'll stop coming; or they'll act better if they do come."

"What's the plan?" I asked.

"First, hit them where it hurts most, and where they hit and hurt us most."

"Bomb their rollers!" everyone shouted.

"You got it! Follow me to the parking lot."

Nearly all of the crowd went along. We perched on tree branches above parked cars.

"You all know what to do. Ready, aim, fire!"

We pooped all over those rollers. Then Haw! Haw! Haw! We laughed as we ascended from the trees like one mighty black cloud.

We split into groups and committed various acts of sabotage. Some birds picked up cigarette butts from the sand and dropped them into unguarded beverage cups and plates of food.

Some crows sneaked up to beach blankets while Persons were surfing or swimming. The birds stole dark glasses and cell phones and dropped them in front of moving rollers, where they were crushed like road kill.

I joined a group that went around pecking holes in beach balls and inflatable rafts. Lots of seabirds joined our protest. They crapped all over umbrellas. They stole car keys and dropped them into the sea. Large birds like pelicans tipped over buckets on the piers, and let the bait fish swim free. Even the sandpipers stopped probing the shore for food and began stuffing beach bags with plastic forks, straws, broken balloons, bottle caps, and cigarette lighters.

A female crow called out, "See those plastic kites up there? Let's mob them like we do to flying predators back home."

"Yeah! Mob! Mob! Mob! We'll drive them out of the territory!" chanted others. More and more joined the gangs. They circled the kites and sent one after another crashing into the sand.

Lots of Persons were hopping mad about what was going on. Their day on the beach was no day at the beach. Many packed up and left. Some wanted to leave, but couldn't find their keys. We birds felt we had done good work together.

When I returned to the roost, Maw was waiting. "What have you been up to, Beloved One?" she asked me.

"Nothing much," I said. "Just saving the Ocean."

Oceana

The following day, after we had eaten, Maw and I spotted a crow lying flat on a rooftop with his wings and tail outspread. We recognized the wing tag. It was Nate. We landed nearby and greeted him.

"Oh, good morning!" He seemed surprised and glad to see us. "I'm just catching some rays. Great way to clear out parasites."

"It is," Maw said. "Try it, Darling."

We both fanned our flight feathers and let the warm sunshine clean us. It felt good, but I didn't want to just lie around all day.

"I'm eager to see the sights," I said.

"I'll bet you are, this being your first beach roost. Have you been to Oceana yet?"

"No. What is…?"

I was interrupted by an almost deafening roar and vibration. I jumped. When it subsided, I exclaimed, "What on earth?"

"Not on earth," said Nate. "In the air. A lot of Persons around here call that 'The Sound of Freedom.' Would you like me to show you what it's all about?"

Maw politely declined. She planned to attend a discussion on egg incubation techniques and chick development. She said I could go with Nate. So I followed him until we reached Oceana.

"Down there's Naval Air Station Oceana," he called. "We'll land in those trees."

We perched in the highest branches. "This spot is close enough," he said. "Any closer and the wake turbulence of takeoff would kill us."

"Wake turbulence? What's that?"

"It's disturbance of the air behind the wings. Their wings— not ours."

Before us lay an enormous parking lot where huge rollers were setting with their wings outstretched. I thought they must be sunning to get rid of their parasites.

The wings had marks sort of like the ones on Nate's tag. All the rollers were facing a few long, level streets that didn't seem to connect to any other roads.

"What are those rollers for?"

"Oh, those are Person-made predators. Deadliest birds in the world."

A deep rumble began as one of the rollers moved forward. It travelled down a straight street and halted. It turned slowly, and rolled forward again. Faster, faster, and faster. It would soon run out of road. I thought it would crash.

Instead, it did something incredible. It lifted into the air with a horrifying roar that shook everything. It didn't even flap its wings, but it flew! As it rose higher, it seemed to get smaller and smaller until it was just a shiny spot in the sky.

Then I understood. It was a jet. And it was flying much faster than I could ever hope to. I was stunned. And mortified. I hung my head.

"What's wrong?" Nate asked.

"Me. I'm wrong. Always. About everything."

Nate cocked his head. "How so?"

"I keep making stupid mistakes. I thought some black cows were crows. I thought a turtle was a rock. And I thought a jet was a daylight star with a long white tail."

"Well, you weren't wrong. From high in the air, a black cow looks a lot like a crow. A turtle inside its shell is like a rock. And from down here, a jet in the sky looks just like a twinkling star. Things appear different when you adjust your point of view, don't they?"

"Yes, I guess they do."

"When you want to understand something well, you've got to look at it a lot of different ways. You aren't wrong, Jet. You're just learning something important. It's called perspective."

Congregation

I enjoyed being part of the congregation at the beach roost. It was an opportunity to have fun with other youngsters. We flirted and groomed each other. We teased each other good-naturedly about our various regional accents. We held flying races and practiced aerial acrobatic tricks.

We played games. My favorite was Stick Catch, where one crow carries a stick high into the air and drops it. The others compete to see who can catch it first.

Sometimes we gathered in the trees and practiced alarm and mobbing calls. Crows use those calls when predators are near and defensive assistance is needed. I overheard some women complaining that crows are terribly noisy. We don't consider it noise. To us, it's the Sound of Freedom.

It wasn't all fun and games though. There were plenty of informative discussions to attend. Topics included:

- Selecting a Proper Mate for Life
- Nest Building Essentials: Choosing Safe and Sturdy Materials
- Benefits of Natural Foods and Dangers of Junk Food Diets
- Cooperative Parenting: A Cultural Tradition
- Beginning Toolmaking: Learning from Our New Caledonian Cousins
- Adapting to Challenges of Urban Life
- Mimicking Alarm Calls of Other Birds for Fun and Profit

Participating in the congregation's activities was an important part of my youth. I felt more confident and had a better sense of group identity. But the best outcome of the trip was that Nate and Maw decided to become mates. When the roost was over, Nate flew back with us to Owenasa.

It was good to be home, and I could hardly wait for the flower buds to bloom again. Then the eggs would arrive and my little brothers and sisters would hatch.

4

Respect

Snow Day

Winter was nearly over. Christmas lights were gone. Days were getting longer. Green blades poked up from the ground where the Morgan girls had planted daffodil bulbs. But late one day, the air grew suddenly cold, and it rained. Everything was drenched. By night, a frigid wind had turned the water hard and slick. All that had been wet was encrusted with ice.

Then it snowed. Flakes as big as dogwood petals silently stacked layer on layer. By morning all grass, roads, leafless tree branches, evergreen boughs, and rooftops were coated with white.

It was quiet. Yellow school buses did not roll out to carry children away. Cars moved slowly, as if trying not to hit snow-flakes that danced in the beams of light in front of them.

I had seen snow before, but none like this. As the lacy flakes drifted down, gray smoke drifted up from chimneys. Where there is smoke, there is warmth, I thought. I flew to a house and rested on the edge of the chimney. The heat warmed me, and the sooty fumes drove parasites away from my feathers.

While I was preening, I heard voices from below. A man was speaking. He said, "Wait, son. Let Daddy zip up your galoshes. There. Now let's get your hands into your mittens. OK. Now we're set."

The man and a little boy stepped out from under the porch roof. Their boots made a crunching sound. They were dressed in puffy clothes that made them look fat. A hat stretched over the boy's head covering all his hair.

His father scooped up a double handful of snow and formed it into a ball. He handed it to his son. The child gazed at it with wide open eyes. He seemed astonished. So was I! I had no idea snow could do that. It was magic!

The child looked from the snowball to his father and laughed. His father laughed, too. He made another snowball and tossed it a short distance. The ball vanished into deep snow.

The father told the little boy to throw his snowball. The boy looked at the snowball and held it close. He shook his head. "Mine!" he said. I didn't blame him. Why throw away such a magnificent orb?

The father made a larger snowball. "If you throw that one," pointing to the ball in the boy's hands, "I'll give you this big one." After a pause, the boy tossed the ball into the snow and reached up for the bigger one.

Forming another ball, the father rolled it in the snow. The snowball grew larger and larger. It was even bigger than the first two. He stopped growing that one, and made another bigger than all the rest. That one, he left on the ground. He stacked the others on it, with the smallest one on top.

He reached into his pocket and got out some buttons. He shoved two big blue ones into the ball on top. Then he put five red ones in a line under those. "There!" he said. "There's a snowman for you. See, he's smilin' at you."

A woman wearing a bulky jacket with a fur-trimmed hood came out of the house. She held a big hat in her hand. "Snowman needs a hat," she said, as she set it on the top snowball. "Here's a carrot for his nose." She offered it to the boy and he took it.

Father held the boy up and helped him press the carrot into the top snowball under the blue buttons. "Let me take a picture of Andy and Daddy and the snowman." The father held his son beside the snowman. "Smile, Andy." The camera went click.

"Now y'all have been out in the cold long enough. Let's go inside." She took the boy from his daddy.

The little one shook his head and pushed out his bottom lip. His eyes glistened. "Come on. You're cold aren't you?"

He shook his head again.

"Daddy's cold." said his father. "Come on, Andy, let's go eat some soup. Mama will bring you out to sleigh ride later."

As she started back toward the house, Andy stretched his arm toward the snowman. He pointed at it with his mitten and said, "Daaah-dee brrrr no-mah." Then, patting his chest with both hands, and giving a little bounce, he exclaimed, "ME!".

"That's right!" his mama agreed. "Daddy built a snowman for you." She held Andy's hand and waved it. "Bye-bye, Snowman," his mama said for him.

Andy did not say 'bye-bye'. I couldn't blame him. I wouldn't say it either. After they went inside, I pulled out one of the snowman's shiny blue eyes, and sat on his hat playing with it.

Snow had stopped falling. The sky cleared. Sunlight glistened on all the pristine surfaces as far as I could see. All was pure and serene.

A big black dog came bounding out of the house wagging his tail. His pink tongue lolled out the side of his mouth. He ran straight to the snowman, lifted his leg, and peed on it.

Ice

The pee made a yellow stain on the bottom snowball. The dog ran in a wide circle through the yard. It drove its snout into the snow, plowing furrows through it. Dog rolled on its back with its paws in the air and wiggled. It crawled on its belly through the snow. It bit the snow. Shook its head like a rattle. Then it ran in circles again.

Now the snow was a blotchy, rutty ruin. The snowman seemed to be sweating a bit. Icicles along the edge of the roof began to drip.

The dog stopped his frenzy. He sniffed the air and stared at something in the front yard that was out of my line of vision. He barked maniacally at whatever it was. In a flash, he bolted and galloped toward the place where his gaze had been focused.

I dropped the button and leaped from the snowman's hat into the air. As I flew just above the dog, I could see a deer in the distance. It was standing on a smooth, flat blanket of snow unmarred by dog. I recognized it as my friend, Dewy! He raised his white tail and turned to run away. Then he dropped out of sight into the snow.

Dewy's soaking head popped up into view again. He wasn't in snow. He was in water! A look of terror was in his eyes. He thrashed frantically, and tried to pull himself out of the water, but the ice kept breaking away from his hooves. He bleated pitifully.

As the dog raced to him, Dewy struck out with his legs. It was futile. He could not gain a footing. He could not fight off the charging dog. My heart ached to see my young friend's life come to such a brutal end.

The snow-covered ice broke under the dog's weight. He swam toward the panicked deer. The dog grabbed Dewy by the front leg and dragged him through the water. Dewy cried for mercy, fearing the dog's teeth more than he feared drowning.

A strong swimmer, the dog pulled Dewy along to where the ice was firm. He clambered onto the ice and grasped Dewy by the back of his neck. Struggling now to gain traction, the dog heaved backward until he had dragged the deer onto solid ground. He released his grip.

The deer lay like a limp rag before the panting dog. Dewy didn't appear to be breathing. The dog shook himself, spattering snow with muddy droplets. He pawed at Dewy and nudged him with his snout.

A distressed voice cried out, "Please, please don't kill him! He's just a baby. He's never been here before, so he didn't know there was a pond. Please don't kill my brother!"

It was Juniper. I hadn't even noticed him until then.

Banjo

"Why?" The dog panted heavily. "Why would I kill him? I'm trying to save him. I knew he was going to break through the ice. I barked to warn him, but he didn't listen. I'll lie on him. Maybe I can warm him up."

He lay down on Dewy and licked his face. "Come on, little fella. Breathe. Come on now. Show us you're OK."

Dewy coughed twice. He shook his head. "Don't be scared of me, little friend," the dog whispered. "I won't hurt ya'. I wouldn't hurt anybody who isn't a flea." He stuck out his tongue and smiled a big, goofy smile.

Juniper bounded to his brother's side and licked him all over. "I thought I was gonna lose you, Knob Head." They both thanked the dog.

Dewy said, "I thought dogs are our enemies."

"Well, some dogs can be pests to deer. But not dogs like me. I'm a Labrador Retriever. An English Labrador Retriever to be precise. We love everybody. We're called retrievers because we're bred to bring things back. The Persons in my family," he pointed his nose toward the house, "just love for me to bring things back to them.

"They throw sticks, balls, frisbees, batons, and squeak toys just to watch me bring them back. It makes them so happy when I do that. They could throw things all day. I have jumped into this pond more times than a dog can count to bring back things they throw in. I was pretty confident that I could retrieve you. But you sure didn't make it easy."

Dewy apologized.

The dog wagged. "I'm just glad all my practice paid off today."

"Me too!" Dewy said. He stood up and started to walk. He limped a little.

"Sorry if I hurt your leg, little fella. But, I had to get a firm grip to get you out."

"I'll be OK. It's just a little sore."

Curiosity was killing me. I had to ask. "That little boy, Andy—is his mama's name Elaine?"

"Yes," said the dog. "Do you know her?"

"Maybe. Does she have a brother named Kevin?"

"Yes. Oh! You must be Kevin's crow! A while back, I heard her say that Kevin wanted to borrow my old puppy crate for his pet crow."

I cringed. "I am not Kevin's pet! He and I have parted ways. I am a free bird now, and I mean to stay that way."

"I see," said the dog. "Well, I understand that being a pet doesn't suit every animal. It's a good life for me, though."

I changed the subject. "Andy's gotten a lot bigger since I saw him last."

"True. Person babies grow fast once they get their feet under them. I think Elaine's going to need that old crate back again. She's getting a new puppy. I'm so excited!"

"I feel sorry for it. I hated being in that crate! Who told you she's getting another dog?"

"Nobody really. But I overheard her say that they'll be getting a new member of the family next summer." The dog cocked his head. "Wait. Maybe…maybe she didn't mean a baby dog."

"You think she means a baby Person?" Juniper asked.

"Could be. Either way, it'll be lots of fun for me! Baby Persons are so cute. They drool just like I do when I see food. And they smell wonderful! Especially when their diapers are dirty."

A man's voice called from the house. "BAAAAAN-JOOOH"

"That's Elaine's husband Ted calling me."

"Your name is Banjo?"

"Yep. Elaine named me that 'cause Ted plays banjo in a roots music band," the dog explained. He sniffed the air. "Gotta get going, he's put food out for me!" Banjo started to run toward the house.

"Save some for me," I called.

He stopped and looked back. "No way!" he said. "I don't love everybody that much!" Off he dashed. A dog of boundless energy with a heart as pure as snow.

Cold Blooded

Days were growing longer. I was on a reconnaissance flight through an unfamiliar gorge where I could stay out of the chilly winds. I discovered a clear body of water on the forest floor. There were no plants growing in it. No fish. No water flowing in or out. So, it wasn't a real pond, just a pool of melted snow with lots of dead leaves in the bottom.

There was something peculiar about it. Floating near the edge was a great cluster of strange-looking bubbles. I landed nearby to investigate.

"Looking for a snack, are you?"

The tiny creature who had spoken had no feathers, fur, or scales. Its bulging eyes were surrounded by a dark mask. Its broad mouth had a thin, white upper lip. Two muscular hind legs were folded along its sides. Two small feet were planted firmly in front of it.

"No. I was just curious about these weird-looking bubbles. Who are you?"

"I'm their mother."

"I don't understand."

"Obviously. Those are not bubbles. They're my eggs."

"So many! Wow! That's incredible!"

"We have a high mortality rate. Lots of the babies won't make it out of here alive."

"How will you feed all your babies?"

"I won't. Tadpoles don't need to be fed."

"But where are the egg shells?"

"Wood frog eggs have no shells."

"Oh! You're a wood frog! I've heard of you."

"I'll bet you thought you were hearing ducks."

"Actually, yes. Maw explained that the quacking was wood frogs."

"Right. That's the way the fellows call us girls to come out and mate. I just unfroze two days ago, and had to hop a long way to get here in time. I'm about worn out."

"Excuse me, did you say you 'unfroze'?"

"Right. I've been frozen all winter. Solid as an icicle. As soon as water freezes, so do wood frogs. We stay that way until the spring thaws."

"I don't think I've ever met anyone who has that talent."

"You haven't. We have a great system. No need to dig a burrow or find a cave to hibernate in. We just crawl under some leaf litter, and wait until the weather warms. Well, I'd better hop off now. It'll be late before I get back home."

"But, if you leave now, who's going to guard your eggs?"

"They'll be fine. No fish in there to eat them."

I looked carefully into the pool. "I think I do see some very tiny fish."

"No, you don't. Those are some other frogs' tadpoles. They must have been laid sooner than mine, and they've already hatched. Look closer. You'll see that they're different from fish."

"Oh, you're right! They have no fins or scales. But, they don't look much like frogs. Although, I have to admit I didn't look much like my parents when I first hatched."

"Before this pool dries up in the summer, the tadpoles will have lost their tails and gills. They will have grown legs. They'll be able to breathe air. They'll end up looking just like me."

"So, will you come back then?"

"Nope. I won't return until next breeding season."

"But...who's going to teach your babies to do wood frog things? How will they learn to hop, find food, avoid predators, freeze themselves for the winter, and find their way back here to mate?"

"They come pre-programmed. They'll know all that from day one. Our only problem is knowing whether next season this pool will be here as a clean, safe place to breed. Nowadays, when you hop into a puddle, you don't know what you're getting yourself into."

"What do you mean? It's just water, isn't it?"

"Water and who-knows-what else. The Persons are always trying to kill weeds and insects. So they're always finding new poisons to spray on the ground or into the air. Where do you suppose those toxins end up? Right here in these vernal pools— our babies' cradles.

"Not only that. Some selfish Person might come along and decide to fill in or drain our pool. If these vernal pools disappear, we'll all croak!"

As the wood frog talked, she became agitated and began hopping about frantically.

"But do Persons care? No! They are always trying to move or remove water to suit themselves, never thinking about what anybody else needs. They don't give a dam. That's why they and the beavers are always at loggerheads, too. The fact is, Persons are the most cold-blooded creatures in the world."

Coming from her, that was saying a lot!

Turn Around

Kevin was planting potatoes when his mama came out of the house carrying a basket. She told him Virgil was on the phone. Kevin dropped his hoe and hurried inside. His mama went into the chicken coop. As she was heading back to the house, Kevin came out.

"Mama, Virgil's daddy is dead."

"What? You mean his real daddy?"

"Yes, ma'am."

"Well now. Caleb Jenkins. Bless his heart." Kevin's mama shook her head. "What happened?"

"A few weeks ago Virgil told me his daddy's sister had called. She said his daddy wanted to talk to him and his mama. She told Virgil that his daddy was bad sick and livin' on the streets in Charleston. But he was in a 12-step program and tryin' to git sober.

"Virgil said he did talk to his daddy on the phone, but his mama wouldn't. His daddy apologized for hurtin' them. He asked Virgil to forgive him. Virgil said he forgave him, but he wasn't about to meet with him. They just wished each other the best in the future, and that was that.

"Then Virgil's aunt called again this morning. She told him his daddy had stepped into the street and got hit by a car."

"Had he relapsed?"

"She said there was no alcohol in his blood at the time. But the driver was drunk."

"Well, that's too bad. Just as Caleb was tryin' to mend his ways."

"That's what Virgil said. He said at least his daddy was finally tryin' to do better, and he died sober."

"Did he say anything about funeral arrangements?"

"He just said he and his mama wasn't mournin' so they aren't goin' to the funeral."

"Well…" Kevin's mama pursed her lips. "I guess I can understand. Sometimes people get goin' the wrong way and don't stop til it's too late to turn around."

Apple Blossoms

Construction on our nest began soon after Nate had been introduced to all our relatives and shown around our territory. More than halfway up to the top of Owenasa, was a place where two strong limbs grew straight out like the arms of a Person reaching for a hug. Maw's heart was set on having a home in that sheltering spot near Owenasa's trunk. Nate agreed that it offered a wide view, was stable, and protected from wind.

Crow nests are never reused. Each nest is built especially for the new clutch of eggs. Building them is a family affair. Nate had several years of building experience. He did most of the heavy work and framed up a nest that could accommodate up to six nestlings. Maw lined the round cup inside with soft materials that wouldn't crack shells or pierce tender skins.

My job was to fetch supplies. Based on what we had learned at the roost, Maw and Nate decided to use only natural materials. No trash, no matter how pretty it looked. So I was hauling in twigs, grasses, straw, leaves, mosses, and feathers. I even got some hair from Banjo after Elaine had brushed him. Some of the games I had played at the beach were good preparation for my work. I was comfortable flying and landing with objects of various sizes and shapes in my beak.

Maw felt she had been too hasty in laying her eggs last season. Late freezes had been hard on the family. So this time, she'd wait until the apple trees bloomed.

When the buds finally opened into pink and white blossoms, we were thrilled. Maw laid one egg each day for four days. The shells were blue-green with brown specks. Each was unique and gorgeous. Nate and I took turns feeding Maw and guarding the nest while she was incubating the eggs.

I was eager to meet my new little siblings. But there would be a long wait before the chicks would appear. Then the work of feeding and protecting them would begin and last for the rest of the season.

Maw said that before we all got busy tending to them, I should go out and enjoy my freedom. She knew I had missed a lot while I was cooped up. Since I hadn't seen the Morgan girls since before my trip to the Ocean, I decided to visit their farm.

Every Bloomin' Thing

Granny, Katelyn, and Ashley were dressed in outfits I'd never seen before. They were wearing white gloves and white hats with black veils. All were standing by the boxes where the honeybees live. Ashley took the roof off a hive and carefully pulled out a narrow wooden frame. Bees were clustered all over it. Granny held up a can that blew puffs of smoke near the hive. Ashley studied the frame for a moment. "There she is!" she said. "And there's some eggs here too. Can you see the queen, Katelyn?"

Katelyn searched the congregation of bees. "I see her! Right there she is!" She pointed her finger close to the frame. "Owwwweee!"

"Did one of them git ya?" Ashley asked.

"Right underneath my arm!" Katelyn grabbed the upper part of her arm.

"Well, she won't do it again," Ashley told her.

"I know. 'Cause they can only sting once. Then their stinger pulls out and they die."

Granny said, "Katelyn, let me check. I want to make sure the stinger is out. Looks OK. Over yonder by the crick is some plantain. Go git you some and chew it up. Then rub it on where you was stung. It'll take the hurt out. You know which plant I mean, don't ya'?"

"Yes, ma'am. I'll be right back."

Katelyn wasn't gone long. She came back running and yelling, "Granny, I found a passel of morels over there!"

"Already?"

Ashley smiled. "Our resident mycologist has made a discovery."

"Yes, and there's also fiddlehead ferns, dandelions, and poke!"

"Well now, we can have poke salat and morels for supper. Katelyn, run in the house and fetch a couple of baskets. We'll pick us a mess of greens."

Ashley said, "Makes my mouth water. I'll finish inspecting the hives and come help y'all."

When she was through, Ashley took off her veiled hat. She looked up into the apple tree where I was perched. She smiled and spoke. "Good morning, Jet."

Ashley recognized me and knew my name! I was shocked. My wings fluttered and my heart pounded.

"It's OK. I know you watch us sometimes. I won't ever tell anyone. Enjoy your freedom, little friend." Then, she blew me a kiss, and left. I relaxed. Ashley could be trusted.

Once she had gone, I offered my condolences to one of the bees in an apple blossom near me. I said, "Very sorry for your loss."

"Buzz off. I'm busy," she responded.

"Well, I'm just trying to express my sympathies. That bee who died was from your hive. You knew her, didn't you?"

"She was my sister."

"Oh, my. Will there be a funeral for her?"

"That's a crow thing. Bees don't do that."

"Well, aren't you going to go home and tell your mother about the tragedy?"

"The queen won't care. Look, we aren't a family. Crows have families. Honeybees have colonies. With us it's 'One for All' not 'All for One.'

"My sister was a guard. Her job was to protect the colony. She was killed in the beeline of duty. Happens all the time. None of us is important. Only the colony matters. The colony must survive.

"Every bee has a job. The queen's job is to lay eggs. If she doesn't do her duty, we kill her and make another queen. The drone bees are males, and their duty is to fertilize the queen. When they've done their job, we kick them out. The rest of us are workers.

"We do all the other work. We make the wax and build the comb. We clean the cells, and heat and cool the hive. We bring in nectar and pollen from flowers and make honey for our food. We feed the babies. We decide which babies will be drones and which will be workers or queens.

"It just depends on what the colony needs. Nobody needs any of us, but everybody needs the colony."

"I see. Being a bee is really different from being a crow."

"There's a lot of pressure on us. Beekeepers like the Morgans are a big help. We don't mind sharing some honey with them. They keep their garden without using pesticides that would kill us. They also help protect us from deadly parasites."

"Crows get parasites, too. They suck."

"Right. But if it weren't for beekeepers, we'd die like flies. And if that happens, nobody eats."

"What do you mean? Not everybody eats honey."

"It's not about the honey. It's about the pollen. Look around. See all those flowers?"

I scanned the area. The grass, trees, and gardens held an abundance of flowers. Service blossoms, dogwood, apple blossoms, blueberry blossoms, dandelions, coltsfoot, mustard, forsythia, henbit, dead nettle, redbud, and violets. "There are so many!"

"And there will be many more in the days ahead. The morels and ferns that the Morgans are collecting now don't need us. But every bloomin' thing does! If we don't get into those flowers and move that pollen around, those plants won't be able to make fruits. No fruits, no seeds, no grains. No food. Everybody starves. Get it?"

"I understand now."

"Nice that a crow does. It's a just a shame more Persons don't. They can't poison all the flowers and expect to survive. To bee or not to be? That is the question."

Crossing

One morning, the sisters were together on Charry Ridge. Sunshine splashed through the early leaves, and the girls' faces were spotted with light and shadows. They were watching the place where Ashley had set apples, grain, and salt blocks.

Dewy and Juniper came out to the feeding spot and began snacking. Dewy was limping. His leg hadn't fully healed after the accident at the pond.

Ashley whispered, "See, Katelyn. Dewy's hurt. He's been limping for weeks. He sleeps real close to this spot. Juniper's been looking after him. Juniper comes out first by himself to see if there's food here. He doesn't eat by himself, though. He goes back and brings Dewy. That way, Dewy can rest, unless it's sure there's a good enough reason to get up."

"Oh, that is so sweet. Juniper is a good big brother," Katelyn said in a hushed voice.

"He is. He knows that if Dewy's leg doesn't heal, he'll be easy prey for coyotes or bobcats. Their mama is busy right now. She's lookin' after her new fawn."

"I hope she got a little girl this time."

After the brothers had finished eating and licking the salt block, they disappeared into the brush. Then Katelyn began wandering around with a small book in her hand. She would find a pine cone and look into the book. Then she would examine a tree branch or its bark or a leaf. Each time, she would look through the book again.

"Ashley, thanks for loanin' me this tree identification book. I'm gonna keep practicin' til I know every tree on this place by name."

"I'm sure they all know you by now."

"I hope so." Katelyn gazed up to the treetops and spread her arms wide. "I love these trees! Every one of them. And my very favorite is that big ole white pine. You know the one?"

"Oh, yes. She's very special. She's home to a lot of crows, you know. They like to nest there."

"You think that old tree was alive when Indians was here?"

"Probably. I'm sure she was when the chestnut trees were still here."

"Chestnut trees? There was chestnut trees here?"

"There's some chestnut wood in the walls of our house. I'll show you. A lot of fences around here is made of chestnut. All these mountains once were covered with American Chestnuts. They were the dominant deciduous tree in the forest. Animals and people ate the nuts. Mountain folks used to gather and sell them. Chestnuts were shipped by train to the cities. Those nuts were a good source of income for a lot of people around here."

"How come they ain't here no more?"

"A lot of the trees were taken for lumber. But mostly they were killed by disease almost a hundred years ago. A mycologist in New York discovered that it was caused by a fungus. Nothing could stop the disease from spreading. Nothing could cure a tree that got sick. It killed almost every American Chestnut tree in the United States. That was real hard on people and forest animals."

"Wow! To think that our tree seen all them other trees die like that. It must have been so sad."

"I suppose so."

We all heard the sound of footsteps, rustling brush, and the rattle of something metal. The girls stopped talking.

As the footsteps got closer, I saw the tip of a fishing rod, then a cap, then a face. It was Virgil! He was carrying a tackle box. When he saw the girls, he looked surprised.

"Oh, hey! I was just on my way to Kevin Ramsey's house on the other side of the ridge. We're goin' fishin' in his sister's pond. Hope you don't mind me cuttin' through here."

"Oh, you're fine, long as you just walk and don't disturb anything. Don't be ridin' any ATVs across Charry, though." Ashley told him.

"I won't. I don't ride them no more. I ride horses now, but only on our farm."

Katelyn's eyes opened wide. "You got ridin' horses?"

"Well, they belong to my stepfather. How's your puppy?"

"How'd you know I have a puppy?"

"I was in the office when you and your granny brought her in."

"What was you doin' in Dr. Duran's office?"

"He's my stepfather. I help out at the animal clinic after school sometimes."

"Oh. Well, that puppy ain't really ours. Somebody dumped her by our house. Granny took her for a check up. She had worms. If we can't find a home for her, we'll take her to the Humane Society. She's too curious about our chickens, so we ain't keepin' her."

"I see. I know some people that hunts rabbits. I'll see if any of them wants a nice Beagle pup. Well, gotta be gittin' on. Kevin's waitin' for me. Thanks for lettin' me cut across."

"Sure," Ashley said.

"Good luck." Katelyn said.

Virgil headed up toward the crest of the ridge and was soon out of sight. Katelyn whispered, "He's cute, ain't he?"

Ashley grinned. "Y'all are both cute."

She paused a moment and said, "Katelyn, if you're ever up here in the woods by yourself when one of them boys crosses the ridge, you'll come straight home, won't you? Don't stay and chat."

"Why?"

"It would be…considerate of you to come on home."

"You think them boys ain't nice?"

"Oh, they both seem to be good kids. I never heard otherwise. Have you?"

"No." Katelyn looked sideways at her sister. "Ashley, is it because you think boys has got only one thing on their mind?"

"No. I don't think that at all. Everybody has lots of things on their mind. But there's one thing that's always on a boy's mind. That ain't their fault, but it sometimes causes them to behave in ways that… well, that might not be the most respectful. You want folks to treat you respectful, don't ya'?"

"Sure, I do."

"Well, sometimes you have to help people with that. Don't put people into situations that make it hard for them to be their best self."

Katelyn lowered her head. "Okay."

"And you also don't want to put yourself into situations that make it hard for you to be your own best self. Right?"

She shrugged. "Right."

"Katelyn… if you disagree with me, maybe you should talk with Granny about this."

Katelyn faced Ashley and shook her head. "I don't need to. You ain't as old as Granny, but you're wise. I'll mind what you say. I think it's kinda like Do Unto Others, ain't it?"

Ashley nodded. "That might be a right way to look at it."

Mars

I was in a service tree, enjoying the first ripe berries of the mountains. On the boulder below me, I heard a ruckus. There a venomous copperhead and an enormous rat were locked in mortal combat.

The snake delivered a toxic strike. The rat continued to scuffle and bite. Suddenly, the snake went limp, and the rat began tearing into its flesh.

I flew down to congratulate the rat on its remarkable victory. Landing right behind it, I declared in a loud voice, "The winner and champion!"

Instantly, the rat dropped dead. It lay curled on its side, its mouth gaping. A thick slime began to drip from its needle-like teeth. Then the stench of rotting corpse hit my nostrils.

"Pee-yew! No winners after all," I said. "The snake and the rat have terminated each other."

The stinking cadaver sprang to its feet and glared at me. "Who are you calling a rat?" it demanded.

I was shocked. I stammered, "I…uh… Well, you of course. You are the biggest rat I've ever seen, and the liveliest dead one."

"I am not a rat! Not even kin to a rat. This is yet another case of mistaken identity. Happens to us all the time."

"Well, then what are you?"

"I'm an opossum. You can call me Mars. That's what Ashley Belle named me. It's short for Marsupial. I heard her tell Katelyn that opossums are the only marsupials in North America—whatever that is."

"I saw you die. But you're not dead now."

"Oh, that's just a little trick we have. It's called 'playing possum.' We're not real fast, have no shells, our camouflage isn't the best, and we're not the toughest fighters. So when we're in danger, we just play dead. If we stink, predators won't want to eat us. I was just playing possum, because you startled me. Thought you might be a hawk coming to kill me and steal my dinner."

"Well, I must say, that was a totally convincing performance. I've never met an opossum before, but I know a possum joke. 'Why did the chicken cross the road? To show the opossum that it can be done'." The opossum didn't laugh.

"NOT funny! You have no idea how many of us get killed that way. We're mostly nocturnal animals, and every night some of us get run over by rollers. I think they do it on purpose. Persons seem to think we are ugly and scary and dirty rats. But Ashley says opossums are special and should be protected."

"What's so special about you? I mean, aside from your incredible talent as dramatic actors."

"Well, for one thing, we can hang by our tails. Nobody else around here can. For another, unlike foxes or raccoons, we don't catch or carry rabies. And you saw that poisonous snake bite me, didn't you?"

"I sure did."

"We are immune to snake venoms. They can't harm us and we love to eat them. We also eat loads of ticks. They're yummy. Crunchy and full of tasty blood."

"Ticks are an awful bother to my deer friends."

"Tell them to come around. I'll clean off every one of those disease carrying parasites."

"They'll be glad to meet you. Where do you live?"

"Here and there. I don't have a permanent home."

"Then, how do you shelter your young ones?"

"Oh, I just carry them in my pouch."

"What?"

"Yeah. Right here. See?"

The opossum opened a pocket on her belly and showed me a collection of tiny, pink babies quietly nursing inside.

"So I guess when there's a road accident, the entire opossum family is killed all at once."

"Exactly!"

The opossum accepted my apology for the tasteless joke I'd made. "Mars, you really are one of a kind!" I told her. "Sorry for interrupting your meal. Safe travels, my peerless friend!" I grabbed up a few service berries for Maw, and headed home to find something even more incredible than Mars.

Break-In

Before I even reached the nest, Maw met me and cawed excitedly. "Come quick! Someone's breaking in!" When we arrived, she perched on the side of the nest. Nate was on a branch above. Neither spoke to me. Both were gazing intently at an egg. It was cracked.

My heart sank. How could this disaster have happened? We had been so careful to guard the nest. Who could have done this? An owl? A hawk? A squirrel? I wanted to kill whoever had invaded our home and destroyed Maw's precious egg.

My beak gaped open, and I dropped the berries I'd been carrying. Maybe it was my fault. If I'd been here, perhaps the three of us together could have fought off the predator. I didn't know what to say or do.

"Maw, how..."

"Hush. Watch and listen."

I heard a faint tapping sound. A crack in the shell seemed to widen a bit. It parted a little more. I thought I could see a slight movement inside the egg. Then it stopped. I held my breath and waited.

The crack grew longer and wider. Through the opening, the pointed tip of a pink wing pushed out. Now I understood. The chick was alive! It was hatching.

I could hear the egg horn on the chick's beak pecking at the shell. The chick kicked the interior of the shell. With a backward thrust, the little head with bulging, blind eyes broke through. A few more kicks, and the largest part of the egg was pushed away. But suddenly the chick's head dropped. Partly in and partly out of the shell, the frail body lay motionless.

"Is it …?" I couldn't bring myself to say the word.

"It's just exhausted. Hatching is hard work." Nate whispered.

After a considerable rest, the chick squirmed out of the remaining shell fragment. The sight of its scrawny, pink body was glorious.

Watching Maw's chicks hatch, one each day, in the order the eggs were laid, I realized something special about us birds. Each of us has left the shield of confinement and entered into freedom and whatever comes with it. Every bird who has ever lived has first performed this act of strength and courage. I was filled with admiration for us. What heroes we all are!

Ally

Helping Maw and Nate care for the chicks kept me busy. I didn't want Maw to have to leave the nest for anything. Nate and I would make sure she had everything she needed. This season the family was going to be protected.

When the nestlings were asleep and Maw had eaten, Nate told me to take a break. I hadn't seen Virgil since before his daddy died. School busses weren't running that day, so Virgil might be home. I thought I'd fly by and check on him.

As I arrived, Virgil and Dr. Duran's dog Ally were coming back from a run in the woods. Virgil was sweating and Ally was panting. Dr. Duran's car pulled into the driveway, and he stepped out.

"I see you two have been playing."

"We had a race. She outrun me."

"Excellent! Belgian Malinois have a lot of energy, and they require exercise. Wait just a minute."

The doctor stepped into the house and came back with two bottles of cold water. He handed one to Virgil and poured the other into Ally's dish. "It's important you stay hydrated. Her too."

Virgil took a big swallow of water. "Dr. Duran, Muchas gracias for helping me with my Spanish lessons. I got an A on my test today."

"Bravo! Muy bien!"

Ally licked Virgil's hands.

"She's become your friend."

"She's a great dog. You know, I was kinda leery of her at first. I seen on TV how police and military dogs can attack people and won't let go."

"Yes. But Ally is not an attack dog."

"Ain't she the breed you trained in the Marines?"

"Same breed, but from a different line. There are two types of Belgian Malinois. One is called the 'working' line. They are bred and trained for military and police work. But not just attack. They also search for dead and wounded, or for explosives and drugs. Many are killed or injured in the line of duty. Those dogs are great at their jobs, but most don't adjust well to being pets.

"Another group of Malinois is called 'show' line. That's what Ally is. Those dogs are bred and trained for strength and agility. They can do amazing athletic feats and tricks for the entertainment of people. They make excellent playmates. But, if they don't have opportunity to use their intelligence and skills, they can get into trouble. Do you think that is also true for many people, Virgil?"

"Yes, sir. I guess so."

"So although the two lines are the same breed, they have different temperaments to suit different jobs."

"I see."

"You know, Virgil, a man can adjust his temperament to suit different roles in his life. Me, for example. In the Marines, I was trained to be focused and tough. Now I am a healer and a husband. It is more important for me to have empathy, patience, and humor."

"Well, I believe you have all that, Dr. Duran."

"Virgil, I would like to have another role in my life. With your permission, I would be honored to adopt you. To become your legal Papa. How would you feel about that?"

Virgil was quiet for a moment. He cleared his throat and said, "The first time Mama and me come to your office, you told Magic to be a good kitten, 'cause she was lucky to be adopted by a kind and generous person."

Dr. Duran laughed. "Ah, I remember."

"I'd feel real lucky to be adopted by a kind and generous person, and I promise to be a good son to you, Dr. Duran."

"Wonderful! So then, please, call me Papa. Let's go tell your mama."

The boy hugged his new father, and the man hugged his new son.

Longer Days

The sun was waking up earlier and going to bed later. The children quit going to school. They began doing unusual things during a season they called "summer vacation."

First the Ramseys and the Durans went away together to fish for trout in a place called Shenandoah Valley. While they were there, they visited the Luray Caverns and Shenandoah National Park. The boys said it was "awesome fun," especially the caves.

Granny and the girls started selling produce from their gardens at the farmers' market in town. On some evenings Granny and Katelyn went to town and played their fiddles in the park with their friends who played music. While the bands performed, the other Persons danced in a way that made clacking sounds with their feet.

The tall meadow grass seemed to dance, too. It swirled and dipped in the breezes across the pastures. I watched Mr. Ramsey and Kevin drive a tractor over the field, and the grass fell in long rows. When that grass turned golden, they formed it into rolls and stored them in a huge shed. And the grass grew green and tall again.

The Queen Anne's lace, chicory, day lilies, and black-eyed Susans bloomed along the roads and fence lines. Wild blackberries, cherries, and elderberries ripened.

Kevin and Virgil played baseball, and Pap went to every game. One day Pap took the boys to see a NASCAR race at Bristol Speedway. The boys said Kurt Busch was the best race car driver ever, but Pap claimed that there'd never be another like Curtis Turner. "Turner was from right here in the Blue Ridge, and he done his first driving delivering moonshine for his daddy."

Ashley Belle became a driver. Granny gave her driving lessons on the farm. When Ashley got a part-time job at Mabry Mill on the Parkway, Granny rode with Ashley to work and came back alone. Later in the day, she'd go back to the mill.

Then Ashley would drive home. But after Ashley got something called a license, she drove to and from the mill alone. Although her days were always busy, Ashley continued to hike up Charry to draw pictures and feed animals.

School was over for the children, but in our family, lessons for the youngsters were just beginning. I spent these longer days helping my siblings learn to fly, to find food, and to speak crow. They were clever and lots of fun to be around. I hoped that someday we could all travel as a family to the great roost at the beach.

When I was not busy helping with the fledglings, I spent a lot of time at the courthouse. Although I never was able to make sense of drawings and writing, I did understand statues. In front of the courthouse was a statue of a man made of metal. He had a metal canteen on his hip and a broad brim metal hat on his head. Between his feet was the stock of a rifle. His hands were wrapped around a gun barrel that pointed straight up.

Some Persons said the metal man should be taken down or moved to a museum because of what he stood for. But I knew what the metal man stood for. He stood for me to perch on. He couldn't move, and his gun couldn't shoot, so I never let the fact that he was a hunter bother me.

From atop his hat, I had a good view of everything happening on Main Street. I could hear what Persons were saying as they went in and out of the courthouse or sat on benches in the lawn. The courthouse was a peaceful place to be. That is, until the day of rockets and bombs.

Rockets and Bombs

Beside the metal man stands a tall pole. Attached to the pole is a piece of cloth. It has that four-sided shape Persons like to see. This cloth is called a flag. Sometimes it's at the top of the pole; sometimes it's only partway up. If the air is calm, it clings to the pole. When a strong breeze rises, it flaps and snaps like clothes on Granny's line. Most of the time Persons just ignore it. So I was surprised to learn of the very special attention they sometimes give to this flag. Thereby hangs a tale.

Early one morning I saw lots of little flags like it all along Main Street. Some hung from sticks attached to street light poles. That morning more Persons than usual were in town. They were all behaving strangely. Most were dressed like flags! They had flags on their heads, on their shirts, on their pants, and around their necks.

Usually, Persons were going into the courthouse or stores. But today no one was. Instead, they were setting up folding chairs and sitting along the sidewalk, facing into the street. But the street was empty. Not a single car or truck rolled past.

Three girls came up on the courthouse lawn. One had a microphone. They stood below the feet of the metal man. Everyone on the sidewalks stood and looked up at the metal man. I thought they might be planning to take him away, so I flew to the roof of the courthouse and peeked from behind the balustrade.

Everyone put a hand on their chest and started talking. They were all saying the same words at the same time. Then I realized that they were not talking to the metal man, but to the flag! I didn't recognize most of the words they were saying.

Next, the three girls on the lawn started singing a song. Everyone sang with them. The song was something about stripes and rockets, bombs and stars.

After the song finished, I heard drums and horns. Bands around here don't usually include those instruments. But the high school band does. I'd seen them lots of times on the high school football field. Now they were coming down the street. They were followed by some little girls with cowboy boots spinning shiny sticks with their fingers.

Next came some little boys wearing blue uniforms with yellow scarves around their necks. A group of old men dressed like soldiers marched by, stamping their feet. A tractor pulled a wagon full of young women wearing long dresses and glittering rings on their heads. They smiled with very red lips and waved at everyone. Several women rode horses with colorful ribbons braided into their manes.

Then I recognized an old friend. It was Banjo! He wore a goofy grin and a white, red, and blue bow. He pulled a cart with balloons tied to it. Andy was riding inside, and his daddy Ted was walking along behind him.

More and more weird Persons passed through the street. Guys with painted faces, baggy clothes and rainbow-colored hair gave lollipops to children. Bearded men wearing shirts with no sleeves and rags tied around their heads crawled by on motorcycles. They seemed to be racing to see who could ride the slowest.

Some tardy red trucks screamed and flashed spinning lights. The persons who had been sitting on the sidewalks in their folding chairs didn't like the noisy trucks. They started picking up their chairs and leaving. I decided to fly away, too.

Maybe Banjo would know why the Persons had been acting so silly and if they were going to be that way tomorrow. So just after sunset, I went to pay him a visit. Banjo wasn't his usual happy self.

He was curled up by the back door shivering and whimpering. There was food in his dish that he hadn't touched. I'd never seen him like this.

"Banjo, are you sick?"

"No."

"You didn't eat your food. That's not like you."

"I have no appetite. Help yourself if you want."

"Thanks." I gobbled up some of the kibble. "Saw you in town this morning. Why were you pulling a wagon in the street?"

"Oh, Ted built that wagon for Andy. Elaine wanted Andy to be in the parade."

"What's a parade?"

"That's when some Persons dress up and act silly in the street and the other Persons watch. What you saw this morning."

"Is a parade going to happen tomorrow?"

"I don't think so. But tonight there will be skyrockets. My family went to the football field to watch. They did it when I was just a puppy. When the booming started, I got so scared I peed on the floor. Since then, Elaine makes me stay outside on skyrocket night."

In the distance, we heard the first of many loud blasts. A portion of the sky glowed. A fountain of tiny red lights drifted in the dark sky. Each burst of colored sparkles glowed for a few moments, faded away, and was followed by a thunderous boom. Banjo whined, shivered, and howled.

"I'm sorry it's so tough on you. I'll stay here, so you won't be alone."

"You're a pal."

I remembered the song the Persons had sung to the flag. It was something about rockets red glare and bombs bursting in air. Maybe that's what these flashes were.

Things finally got quiet. We heard a roller pull into the carport.

"That's my family coming home."

I heard Ted say, "I just can't believe Andy slept through the whole thing."

Elaine said, "He's had a big day. He's all worn out."

I heard the door shut.

"Oh, why do they do it, Jet? There are so many things to see in the sky every day and night. Colorful sunrises and sunsets, the moon and stars, rainbows, and fluffy clouds. Those things are beautiful and very gentle. Why do Persons put noisy rockets in the sky?"

I recalled what Nate had said about the loud jets at Oceana. "I think maybe it has something to do with the sound of freedom."

"Freedom should try to be more peaceful."

Banjo would never be alone again on a skyrocket night. Elaine used that old puppy crate to bring the "new member of the family" home from a breeder in Roanoke. Her name is Dobro. She looks just like Banjo only smaller and blond.

Snap!

"Fool! Simpleton! You gormless dolt! Dimwitted shlub! You obtuse dumbbell!"

I peered through the branches searching for the source of these insults. At the base of a nearby tree, I spotted a gray fox. He continued to shout epithets.

"You deserve to die, lunkhead! You're too stupid to live!"

"Why do you deride me? You don't even know me."

My remark must have startled the fox out of his rant. He spoke to me politely. "It's true, Crow. I don't know you, and I didn't even know you were there. In fact, I wasn't speaking to you."

"Well, who then? I don't see anyone else here."

"I was addressing my worthless self."

"How have you come to have such a low opinion of yourself?"

Fox raised his front paw. A piece of metal attached to a chain hung from it. "See this leg hold trap? My entire life has been spent on this mountain, so I knew that traps were set for the unwary. I was too clever to step into one, I told myself. But I let myself be lured. Snap! Now I am caught and my life is over."

"Not yet it isn't. Don't give up hope." I empathized with Fox. I knew what it's like to be captured, and how it felt to regret mistakes.

"I have seen what happens to trapped animals, so I know what will become of me. The Person who set the traps will come with a long stick. He will place the end of the stick over my neck and press it to the ground. Then he will pull back my chin. Snap! My neck will break, and I will die. Then the trapper will slice off my skin and carry it away. If he doesn't dispatch me soon, I will just die of thirst. Either way, I am doomed."

"Dreadful! If you promise not to bite me, I can try to release you."

Fox sighed. "I've never enjoyed having to eat crow. I promise I will not harm you."

I pecked and pecked at the trap that held fox's life in its jaws. No use. I pulled at the chain that fastened the jaws to the ground. It wouldn't break or come loose.

"Shh. I hear voices," Fox whispered. "Trappers are headed this way. Hide, Crow! They might kill you and use your carcass for bait. But please stay close. I'm not too foolish to understand that it is a good thing to have a friend, even if one is about to die."

"So, I have heard. I'm your friend til the end, Fox." I hid in a tree branch directly above him and waited.

Clearly, I could hear a man saying, "I purchased all this acreage from a man I met at the VFW. His family had lived on this land for many generations. He has been here his entire life, except for the years he was in the army. Like the rest of his family, he gardened, hunted, fished, and trapped for pelts to sell. He has diabetes now, and has lost his leg. With only one leg and no family, he no longer can he live as before. He needed cash. I was happy to buy this land. It is adjacent to our property, and it is perfect for our herd."

That voice sounded familiar. So did the next one that spoke. "Look over there! I see a fox!" Down the trail came the owners of the voices and the land. It was Dr. Duran and Virgil! I could hardly believe it. I never expected them to be trappers.

Yet Virgil was holding a long pole with a forked end, just as the fox had described. "Good for you, son! Go quickly and hold its head down. I'll take care of the rest." Just as the fox had predicted, Virgil used the stick to press the fox's head to the ground. Dr. Duran forced the trap levers down with his feet. The jaws opened, and he held the fox's paw tenderly.

"Fortunately, his leg is not broken. I think it is safe to let him go, Virgil."

Dr. Duran let go of the paw and backed up. Virgil lifted the pole from the fox's neck and stepped away. The astonished fox looked at them and offered gratitude. The Persons did not understand him. "Shoo! Go on now!" Dr. Duran told him. The fox trotted away.

"He sure is a beautiful animal. Lucky we found him in time," said Virgil.

"There are many more traps to discover. We need to find them and eliminate all hazards before we can release our bison onto this ground. Although the seller cannot live as his ancestors did, the bison will be here again where their relatives once lived."

Jump

It was the season when black walnuts drop to the ground, pumpkins appear on porches, and corn stalks are brown and brittle. I was flitting through the woods, snacking on berries and bugs. Now and then I found a few acorns that squirrels hadn't already taken. Trees were molting, and through the branches I spied my old friends, the whitetail brothers. I lighted on a limb nearby and cawed to them.

"Hey, boys!" They both looked up. I noticed that their antlers had changed. "What's happened to your crowns? They were nice and fuzzy. Now they look like dried bones."

Dewy said, "We've polished them on the trunks of some spicebushes. But I'm afraid the polishing rubbed off their bark as well as our velvet. Spicebush does smell wonderful."

"Not as wonderful as she does," Juniper said. He raised his chin and flared his nostrils.

"She who?" I asked.

Juniper didn't answer. Dewy did.

"He doesn't even know who 'she' is. But my brother's in love with the scent of her. Crazy in love, I mean. Can't think straight. Keeps wandering around, sniffing the air. Putting his own scent everywhere he goes." Dewy shook his head. "He's not himself. He's a mess, I tell ya'."

Juniper spoke. "You're too young to understand what true rut is like. All I can think of is her. Her fragrance is intoxicating. Sweeter than honeysuckle. Sweeter than multiflora roses. I'd follow her anywhere."

Dewy stared at him. "He's bedazzled. Maybe this doe has put a spell on him. She might be a witch."

Juniper snorted and stamped, "Shut up! I won't have you talking that way about the possible future mother of my possible future fawns!" He lowered his head and poked his brother roughly with tips of his antlers.

"Hey!" I squawked. "No need for that!"

Dewy backed up and changed his tone. "Sorry. Sorry. No offense. It's just that you seem to have forgotten what mama said."

"No, I haven't. She said that when the tree branches bud again, I might be a daddy if I find the right doe. We only have a few days left to meet."

"Mama said to stay off the road!"

Remembering the tragic fate of my Paw, I said, "That's very good advice."

Dewy shook his head. "Twice! Twice I've had to stop him from stepping right out."

All the while, Juniper was walking steadily through the forest as if in a trance. We were just tagging along, trying to get him to come to.

"She's nearby," he said. "She wants to meet me."

"Really? Then why does she run away every time you get close to her?"

Juniper glared at Dewy. "She's shy!" He moved forward and sniffed.

From where I was perched, I could see through the branches that Juniper was headed toward a road that was cut into the mountainside.

In a hushed voice Juniper said, "I think I see her in a clearing down there. Yes! Over there. It's her!"

He dashed at breakneck speed down the steep slope. I could see the doe in an opening across the road. Dewy yelled, "I'm telling!"

I could see a car speeding up the hill. Juniper raced ahead to where the bank dropped off at a sharp bend. I stood erect, flapped, and cawed five times—my danger signal. No use. He jumped.

Hit

Juniper actually jumped over the roof of the car. He landed safely in the middle of the road. The car sped on up the hill and disappeared around the bend. A second car heading the other way had crested the hill and was aimed straight at Juniper.

The right front tire hit a pothole. The car jerked sharply to the right, slid on the gravel and lunged over the rim of the road. With a thunderous crash of steel and glass, it smashed into a white oak tree. One wheel spun freely above the ground. The air stunk like burned rubber.

The tree cried out. "I caught it! I stopped it from falling into the ravine, didn't I?"

"You sure did!" I answered. I flew up to the oak and perched. "You took a mighty hard hit. Are you alright?"

"It hurts, but I'll be OK. Check inside the car. The Persons aren't making a sound."

The noise of the crash had startled Juniper out of his trance. He turned back, looked up, and called, "What happened?"

"You were a dumbass! That's what happened!" his brother shouted.

I flew to the hood of the car and peered through the broken windshield. Blood everywhere. No one was moving. I hopped inside for a better look.

"Awwk!" I darted out again. "Juniper, get up here and help!"

"Help Persons? Why should I help them? Reckless drivers. They made me miss my date. Probably just deer hunters anyway. They're everywhere this season."

In a rage, I flew at him, grabbed him by the antlers, and pecked the top of his head.

"Ow! Ouch! Stop!"

"Damn it, you numbskull! Get your white tail up there now, or so help me, I'll peck your eyes out. It's not hunters. It's the Morgan sisters."

"Oh no. Noooo! Ashley and Katelyn." Juniper's voice was raspy. He dropped to his knees.

I had been too harsh with him. So I spoke more gently. "Listen, Juniper, they're hurt, and they need your help. You've got to pull yourself together and come up to the roadside."

He gathered himself and did as I said.

"How can we help?" Juniper asked.

"I can run and get Banjo and Dobro. Maybe they can pull them out," Dewy offered.

"That won't work," I told him. "They're strapped in. We have to get some Persons to help them."

"But Persons won't listen to us," Dewy said.

He was right, in a way. I could talk. I could fly to the nearest Person, tell them the whole story, and plead for help. But they would be so dazzled by the fact that a bird could talk, they wouldn't pay attention to what I was saying. Sometimes words are worse than useless.

"You're right. They won't listen. But we can make them see. We must stop the next roller that comes by." I cawed up to the white oak, "Say, have you got any dead limbs up there that extend over the road?"

"Sure do."

"Well, drop the biggest one you can into the middle of the road."

"I've been meaning to get rid of this heavy one anyway. I'm going to need a little help with it though. A strong wind would be welcome about now."

From the woods below the road, a full-throated roar made us all tremble. Smashing through the undergrowth on the side of the ravine, straight toward the wreck charged a massive black bear.

Drop

"Would a strong bear be welcome?" he asked in a deep voice. "I get awful hungry this time of year, so I was snagging fish down there. Sounded like something exploded. I smelled blood, so I came running." As he spoke, he scrambled up the oak tree. "I overheard you say that the Morgan sisters are in there. I feel sick to think of them being hurt."

"You know them?" asked the oak.

"We've seen each other on Charry Ridge now and then. I never got too close, so I wouldn't frighten them. But I watched them from a distance. Cutest little Person cubs I ever saw. Ashley named me 'Bearnard'."

When he got to the right place in the tree, he called out, "I'll try not to let it hit the car. Here it comes. Look out below!" Standing on the dead branch, Bearnard gripped the tree trunk with his front claws, sank his heavy body downward, and thrust with his back feet.

The limb couldn't support his weight and broke with a sharp crack. It smashed to the pavement with a thump and rustle of dry leaves. Some smaller twigs and branches snapped and scattered across the ground. But the heaviest part had fallen too close to the tree.

Hurrying back to the ground Bearnard said, "I'd better make myself scarce now. When rescuers show up, they might get the wrong idea about what I'm doing here."

"Right." I said. "And that could be dangerous for you."

"You better scat!" Dewy added.

Juniper scowled at him. "Leave it to you to joke at a time like this!"

We all thanked Bearnard for his help.

"Glad to do it," he said. "Hope the girls will be found soon." He scampered into the ravine and across the creek at the bottom.

Juniper and Dewy hooked the branch with their antlers and dragged it into place. Now, it was impossible for a roller to pass.

"That's using your head the right way!" I cawed.

A voice from across the road called out. "Hey, Jet! Maybe I can help too." It was a young raccoon.

"You know me?" I asked.

"You visited our family when I was just a kit. You told us a whopper of a story. Listen, I might be able to blast the horn on that car to attract attention when a Person comes by."

"You know how to blow a car horn?" Dewy asked.

"Sure do. Once a roller broke down on the Parkway. The guy got out and started to walk. The windows were open, so my sister and I climbed inside to check it out.

"We downed his soft drink and a big bag of chips. We chewed up his pack of cigarettes and a candy bar. I was playing with the steering wheel when I accidentally hit the horn. The guy heard it and came running back. He was all pissed. Anyway, if y'all can get a roller to stop up here, I'll hit the horn on that wreck. That should get some attention."

"Worth a try!" I said. "Dewy and Juniper, you stand on the side of the road near the wreck. When a roller comes by, someone will have to get out to move the branch. They'll notice you handsome fellows. When they do, go over the rim toward the crash site. Raccoon, wait til you see the whites of their tails. Then you'll know that Persons have left their car. You hit the horn and then run."

"Got it." Raccoon got in behind the steering wheel. The brothers stood in position. I perched on the dead branch in the road. We waited. We hoped.

Stop and Run

A car traveling uphill arrived at last and slowed to a stop at our roadblock. The right front door and the left back door opened wide. Two boys wearing uniforms got out.

I didn't recognize the car. In those strange outfits, the boys looked unfamiliar at first. But as they approached, I realized that I knew them. It was Virgil and Kevin! I flew up and hid from Kevin among the leaves of the white oak. The boys started toward our roadblock.

"Psst. Kevin, look at them young bucks over here."

Kevin crossed the road and stood by Virgil. Both boys watched as the brothers turned, raised their white tails, and slowly led the way toward the wreck. A car horn blasted. Raccoon scrambled out through the windshield and up the oak. Hearing the horn, the boys peered into the ravine and spotted the car wedged against the tree.

Both boys wheeled around and yelled at the same time. "Mama, come help!" "Mrs. Ramsey. Come quick! There's a wreck down there."

Kevin's mama stepped from the car and ran. She looked to where the boys pointed and said, "You boys stand back. I'll take a look."

"You'll get all dirty, Mama. I'll go." Kevin started forward.

His mother put her arm out in front of him, and he stopped.

"I said stay here!" She stepped sideways down the slope, sliding partway on the leaf litter. When she reached the car, she grabbed the door handle and steadied herself. She jerked the door open, looked inside, and gasped. Covering her mouth, she looked away.

"Dear Lord Jesus! It's the Morgan girls! Kevin, run to the nearest house and tell them to call the emergency squad. Fast as you can now!"

Kevin didn't move. "Virgil's already gone, Mama. His house is about a mile out the road. Are they hurt bad?"

"Yes. But I think they're both alive. Shut off our car engine, and bring me the first aid kit from the trunk, son. I'll try to stop Katelyn's bleeding.

The whitetails, the oak, Kevin, and I watched silently while she worked. Her hands and shirt became bloodstained. She sighed and shook her head. "Maybe I should have driven. I just couldn't bear to leave these two little girls all alone out here. Do you think Virgil can run that far?"

"I know he can. Virgil is the fastest boy on our team. You should've seen him at practice today. Virgil says he always runs like his daddy's still chasin' him."

Mrs. Ramsey pursed her lips. Her brow wrinkled. "Pray with me, Kevin."

The two of them started talking to Heavenly Father, though he was nowhere to be seen. They were asking for help when a car drove up and pulled to the side of the road. I thought it might be him. But no. It was Virgil and Dr. Duran.

"The emergency squad should be here shortly. I'll have a look at the girls," the doctor said.

A few moments later, he clamored up to the roadside and said, "They're still holding on. You did well, Mrs. Ramsey."

"She was a Girl Scout." Kevin told him.

"It's a blessing that limb was in the road. If we hadn't had to stop, we'd never have seen the car," she said.

Dr. Duran offered an alternative hypothesis. "Or perhaps trying to avoid hitting the limb in the road was what caused the accident."

They each had a theory. Neither would have believed the truth.

Rollers with flashing lights came screaming toward the scene. Dr. Duran said, "Hustle, boys. Let's move that branch out of the way."

Lingering

I returned to Owenasa. "You are welcome," she said as she always does when one of us comes back to her. I was exhausted. I closed my eyes. We were quiet.

"I had a visitor," she whispered. "A lovely spirit came to me. It lingered in my branches and became tranquil. Then it moved away."

I opened my eyes wide and stood upright. "Was it a boy or a girl spirit?"

"No way to tell."

"Owenasa, please, tell me which way the spirit went!"

Owenasa breathed sweetness to me. "Dear One," she said. "Even if you fly faster than a jet, you cannot catch a spirit and bring it back. A spirit does not move as the crow flies. It moves in all directions."

I folded my legs and dropped onto my feet again. I tucked my head under my wing and listened to the life flowing from her roots, up her trunk, and out through her branches in all directions.

"Owenasa, my wings are aching. And my heart is…is…singing a song with no words."

"As old as blood. I know," she said. "Stay close to me and rest."

Story Telling

In the days following the crash, the postman stopped putting things in the Morgan's mailbox out by the road. Instead, he carried the mail to their door. Granny and Katelyn had many visitors.

People came carrying bags of groceries. Kevin's mama and Virgil's mama stopped by with flowers and some boxes. Kevin's daddy brought a truck full of firewood. Kevin and Virgil stacked it on the porch and by the shed.

I saw that sometimes Persons act like crows. Just like us, they feed and care for ones who are sick or hurting. Persons do so many surprising things.

My usual method of gaining new information about them is eavesdropping. After the wreck, I learned that many Persons who had not been present at the accident nevertheless had stories to tell about it.

I overheard kids at school bus stops, shoppers on the parking lot of Cox's Market, women coming out of church together, hunters in camouflage sitting around campfires, and people meeting at the green boxes to dump out their trash. The various stories I heard went something like this:

"Just as their car come over the hill, a big ole tree fell across the road and crushed it."

"Kids all run these roads like they think they's the next Curtis Turner."

"Sure is mighty peculiar that the front passenger seat was empty. Somebody else mighta been in that car and run off after the wreck."

"My sister-in-law knows somebody that's got a nephew in the rescue squad. He said looked to him like somebody had drug that tree into the road so it would seem like that was the cause of the accident."

"Ashley mighta been dopin' like her mama done."

In front of Mountain Town Diner, I overheard a woman say a curse had caused the accident. A woman with curly white hair told her story in a wheezing voice to a younger woman as they sat on a bench eating ice cream cones.

"Seems to me like that Morgan family's cursed of the Lord. None of 'em is God fearin' people. That goes way back for generations. I was in high school with Alma Bennett. Her parents was drifters from up north. S'posed to be artists, some kind. I don't believe they was even married. Just livin' in sin is all. They didn't have nothing but Alma. Her own folks up and left her here when they went their separate ways." The woman paused to lick the melting ice cream.

"Oh, she was smart, all right. She went and took up with Glenn and married him just to git aholt of that Morgan farm, I'd say. After Glenn got kilt, she got widow's payments. She worked in that shirt fact'ry for years. Instead of movin' on, she just bided her time, ya see. She just stayed up there with her boy Scott and that old man Spencer. Sinful. Now, her boy is dead and his girl too. So, I'm thinkin' that's just her punishment!"

The other woman nodded and frowned with brown ice cream on her lips. "The house of the wicked is cursed of the Lord," she said.

The Marauder

At Harlan's Garage, a man with a big belly, a thick gray beard, and a thin, gray pony tail told a different story. He approached a man outside the shop who was looking at a newspaper and shaking his head.

"Hey, Leon. Your car gittin' state inspection?" the big man asked.

"Hey, Mr. Shelby. Yeah. And getting new tires. My daughter drives that one to school. I was just readin' about that wreck out on Maxey Mill Road. I graduated with Scott Morgan, and his mama give me fiddle lessons years ago. That poor woman. Lost her husband, child and grandchild."

"Well, I knew Scott's daddy and mama. We was in school together. Me and Glenn and Harlan Jarvis hung out together. All us boys could turn a wrench, you know. When we wasn't workin' on somebody's car or tractor or motor bike, we was talkin' about it.

"I can tell you somethin' about the car that Morgan girl was drivin'. That was a 1964 Mercury Marauder. Glenn's daddy bought it from a guy in Radford. The Marauder had belonged to that guy's son. The son had got wounded in Nam and couldn't drive it no more. Glenn's daddy, Spencer, give him that car for a graduation and weddin' present.

"Glenn and Alma was in love with each other, but we was all in love with that Marauder. Nobody else had nothin' like it. The four of us had some fine times runnin' the roads that summer. Until us boys was drafted. After Glenn got killed, Alma and Spencer wouldn't drive that car. It was put up on blocks in a shed.

"A few months back, Alma called Harlan. She asked could he fix up that old car for Scott's daughter, Ashley. Ashley had got her license and was gonna graduate next spring. All the girl wanted for her birthday and graduation present was her granddaddy's pretty red car out in that shed.

"Is that right?"

"Yessir. Alma said when Ashley was just a little bitty thing, she'd to go to the shed and set in that car, pretendin' she was drivin' it. Her feet couldn't even touch the pedals.

"Well, of course, Harlan was pleased to do it. He said the car was in good shape. He tuned it up and retrofitted it with seatbelts. The air condition wasn't workin' but Ashley didn't care about that, just long as the heater worked. So, Harlan got it all ready for her. When her and Alma come to pick it up, Ashley was real tickled. She thanked Harlan and give him a big hug.

"But here's the thing. That Marauder was heavy—4,200 pounds of muscle car. That was a lot of weight for them original drum brakes to hold back. I believe the car just got away from that little girl when she tried to stop it comin' down that mountain. Front end crumbled like a crushed beer can."

Leon said, "It's a dang shame. Ashley was in class with my daughter Bethany. She said the kids and teachers is all grievin'. Bethany says Ashley was real smart and a gifted artist. She had drawn sketches of every senior in the school. The kids are bringin' them back in. They all want them included in the year book along with their class pictures."

"That's a real nice idea."

A thin man appeared at the garage door, wiping his dirty hands on a blue rag. He said, "You're all set" and went back inside.

"Okay. Thanks, Mr. Jarvis."

Mr. Shelby said in a hushed voice, "Listen. You might better not speak with Harlan about any of this. When I told him the little girl had passed away, he… Well, it 'bout tore him up."

Leon nodded, and went inside. I heard him say in a loud, cheery voice, "Well, Mr. Jarvis. How much do ya' owe me for your work?"

"Heh, heh, heh. Here's the bill, Leon. Just pay me what I owe ya."

Katelyn's Story

Every day I went to the Morgan house to check on Katelyn. She wasn't getting on the school bus yet, and she never came outside.

When at last I did see her, she was slowly descending the porch steps with two long sticks under her arms. She used those sticks like extra legs. She kept one of her real legs bent so her foot was off the ground.

I perched on the rail of the upstairs porch and watched her. Katelyn hobbled to a bench where she and Granny had often sat playing their fiddles and singing. She stayed very still. That was most unusual for Katelyn. Her eyes were closed. For a long time she sat that way.

Granny came outside carrying a pink sweater. "Katelyn, you been out here a while. Ain't you cold, honey? Here."

"Thanks, Granny." Katelyn pulled the sweater on. "It was real kind of Mrs. Duran to knit this for me. So nice and soft, and my favorite color too."

"Yes, and it fits you fine. Are you hurtin' Katelyn? You need some pain medicine?"

"No, thanks. My leg was achin' me a bit, so I come out here to meditate, like Daddy said he done. My therapist taught me. I asked her to."

"I see. And that's helpin' you?"

"It is. Sit by me, Granny." She patted the bench.

Granny said, "I forgot that Mrs. Duran left this little package for you, too. She said it's from Virgil."

Katelyn tore off the wadded brown paper. "Oh! A puppy." She read the note inside. 'Hey, Katelyn. I hope you are feeling better. Here is a pup that won't mess with your chickens. Virgil'. This looks just like that puppy we took to the vet last spring."

"It does! Mrs. Duran told me Virgil made that for ya' with some wood carvin' tools he had got for his birthday. He is a real talented wood carver."

"That was real thoughtful of him." Katelyn wrapped the paper back around it. "Granny, I been startin' to remember things about the accident."

"You have?"

Katelyn nodded. "We was at the library."

"That's right."

"Ashley and me turned in our books and videos and got some new ones. We was walkin' back to the car, and I told Ashley I wanted to ride up front this time, like you do when you ride with us. She never let me sit in front. She said no again.

"I asked why. She said 'cause she'd like to pretend she's Hoke, and I'm Miss Daisy."

Granny smiled at that.

"I said well I want to be Hoke, and she said, 'When you git your driver's license, you can be Hoke and I'll be Miss Daisy. Until then, I'm Hoke.' I said, 'You treat me like a baby sometimes.'

Katelyn continued, "Ashley opened the door for me. I got in the back seat. We was headin' back here to the farm, and Ashley said, 'It's mighty quiet in this car, Miss Daisy. Sure would be nice if you'd sing us on home.'

"Well, we was ridin' along the river then, and so I begun singin' 'Down to the River to Pray.'

"The next thing I remember is…a funny dream. I dreamed we was headin' home, and a crow and a deer and a raccoon and a big ole bear was drivin' our car. Ashley was drawin' their picture. And I said, 'Ashley Belle Morgan, why are you lettin' all them wild animals drive this car, but you won't even let me sit in the front seat?'"

Katelyn started to laugh. Then her face seemed to crumble and tears slid down her cheeks. She rested her head on Granny's shoulder. Granny pulled her closer, stroked her hair, and kissed her head. She took a handkerchief from her pocket and handed it to Katelyn.

Katelyn wiped her eyes, "I know Ashley was jokin' about wantin' to play Drivin' Miss Daisy. She just wanted me to sit in the safest seat, in case…"

"Yes, she did."

"Granny, at the end of that movie, Miss Daisy told Hoke he was her best friend. Ashley was my best friend."

"She was. And you were hers. When Ashley first come here to live, she was leaving her home and daddy and her little school friends. I worried that she'd be awful downhearted bein' left here. But first thing she done was run straight in the house and ask me 'Where's Katelyn?' I said you was havin' a nap, and I showed her where you was sleepin'. She petted your head real gentle and whispered, 'I got my sister back.' Then you opened your eyes and told her, 'I was playin' possibly.'"

Katelyn smiled. "I meant 'playin' possum' didn't I?"

"You did. And Ashley understood that. She slapped her hands on her knees and laughed. She said, 'My sister said a joke.' I had one of the bedrooms all fixed up for Ashley, but she wanted to stay in the same room with you. I believe Ashley would've had awful hard times if it wasn't for you. You was a great comfort to her."

"Thanks for tellin' me about that."

"I'd like you to remember something, Katelyn. Your sister's last wish was to hear you sing. I hope you'll keep right on singin' for her."

Katelyn nodded. "I will."

Crown

On the day Ashley's body had been buried in the family cemetery, I'd watched until all the Persons had left. After the sun had settled in its nest, the sky glowed pink. Against it, bare tree branches seemed like flat black lines that Ashley's magic pencil might have drawn. Then I began to caw to my flock.

In small groups they came and settled into trees near the burial ground. When all were assembled, the branches had been filled with crows as they had been full of leaves. We had held a funeral for our friend, as we'd have done for one of our own.

The crows had lamented in chorus. They had sung of Ashley's gentle and generous ways. Each bird who had witnessed her acts of kindness spoke fond memories of her faithful presence in the forest. That night we stayed together, mourning until morning.

Later, after all the Christmas decorations in town had disappeared, a couple of men set a white stone on Ashley's grave. Both the stone and the grave were that awful four-sided shape I detested. But it didn't really matter. I knew her spirit had left all those shapes behind. She is in that unbreakable circle.

As soon as their truck left, I saw Juniper step from the shadows of the forest with his head down. He walked to Ashley's grave and struck his antler on the stone again and again.

I perched on a gravestone nearby and asked, "What are you doing, Juniper? Have you lost your mind again?"

He shook his head hard. The antler dropped off. He knocked the other antler until it fell onto the grave.

"No," he said softly. "It's time for my crown to come off. I just wanted to give it to her. I don't deserve it anyway."

"Juniper, Ashley would have forgiven you. You must forgive yourself. No one gets through this life without making mistakes."

Downy feathers of snow began to fall. The gathering flakes transformed the countryside. Here and there, something peeking out from the cover hinted of what had been before. Just so, the days drifted by, gathered, and gradually changed all I had known in my youth.

5

Fulfillment

Transformations

Owenasa and the Ocean had prepared me to expect changes. Some brought me joy. Others, sorrow.

One bright day, I saw a plume of black smoke rising from Ramsey's meadow. Curiosity drew me to it. Old Flora had died in her house. Mr. Ramsey had set the place on fire. He stood for a long time, watching the flames and talking quietly with his son. When they left, only a black heap and a stone chimney remained.

Days followed nights. As days grew long, nights grew short. When nights lengthened, days were brief. The moon got fat, then thin, and fat again. Flowers bloomed and faded away. Trees budded and filled with leaves. They fell and left branches bare. Over and over these things passed before my eyes. Other changes came with them.

Kevin and Virgil graduated from high school with honors. Kevin went away to something called college in a place called North Carolina. I didn't see him again. I didn't miss him.

After graduation, Virgil trained as an EMT and drove an ambulance. One day, I overheard his pap tell Dr. Duran that he had terminal pancreatic cancer. Pap said, "I guess I look like I ain't got much. But I never did need much. After my Ina Mae passed, I sold our farm. With the proceeds and her life insurance, I bought this here house trailer and made some good investments. I saved some from my pension checks, too.

"Ever thing I have will go to Virgil. He's grown into a good man. You had a lot to do with that. And I want you to know how much I appreciate all you done for my daughter Mandy and him. You been..." Pap's voice broke. He wiped his eyes. "You been a blessin' to us all, Mateo."

Virgil quit driving ambulances. He moved in with Pap. After Pap died, Virgil went away.

When the right season came, my mate and I found each other. Together we built our nests and raised our broods. Each of our offspring is known to us as Dear, Precious, Darling, and Beloved. Each has our unending love, and we are deeply grateful for them.

Mateo Duran took a partner in his veterinary clinic. He stays home more often now to tend his herd of twenty bison. Virgil's mom, Mandy, helps him. She also keeps her own herd—of cats. She calls them Midnight, Misty and Marigold. I'll let you guess what colors they are.

Katelyn got her wish to perform at the Fiddlers' Convention. She wrote a song called "Magic Pencil" and it won a prize. She and Granny recorded something called albums. Katelyn writes books, too.

Long after his disappearance, Virgil returned. Now, there are two Doctor Durans in town—one for Persons and one for other animals. Katelyn and Virgil got married, and they live in the old house with Granny.

Oxymoron

Fiddle music was in the air, so I drifted along with it to the Morgan farm. There was Granny, seated alone on the bench in front of the house. She played a few tunes, then placed her fiddle into a fiddle-shaped box. She set the box and her bow into the car and shut the door.

Virgil and Katelyn came outside. They both hugged Granny. She said, "Now, don't expect me back til this evenin'. We'll be playin' at the Blue Ridge Music Center all afternoon. I'll come straight home after that. Sure wish you could come with me, Katelyn, but I know you'd better stay here today."

"I'll soon be back to performin' with y'all, Granny. Y'all have a wonderful time. Give the other band members my love."

"I surely will do that, honey. Bye."

"Love you!" Virgil and Katelyn said together as Granny got into the driver's seat. They waved until the car was out of sight.

"Such a beautiful morning, Virgil. I'd like to go for a walk."

"Sure. Where to?"

"Let's go up to the cemetery."

They joined hands and passed through the gate where the daffodils were blooming. They started up the path. I decided to fly up ahead of them. When they arrived, Katelyn and Virgil parted ways. She went to where Scott and Ashley were buried. Virgil wandered around, looking at headstones toward the back of the graveyard.

"Katelyn, honey, come look here at this marker," Virgil called.

"Be there in a little minute." Katelyn was standing by Ashley's grave. From the pocket of her long skirt, she took something, and set it gently on the headstone. She covered it with her hand, closed her eyes and smiled. Then she walked across the cemetery to her husband.

Curious, I flew down to see what Katelyn had left behind. It was a fairy stone.

"Says this man, Eamonn Morgan, was a soldier in the War Between the States—on the Union side!" Virgil said. "You know anything about him?"

"Oh, yes! He was my very, very great grand uncle. We know lots about him. Granny has letters that he wrote home. I'll show 'em to you if you like."

"I'd find that interesting. How'd he end up in the Union Army? Was he livin' up North?"

Katelyn shook her head. "No. He was livin' right where we are now. At that time, Eamonn was the only male in this family that was of age to serve in the military. But he was not willing to turn against the United States. He said his forefathers had fought to build this nation, and he would never fight against his own country. He thought if the Union was broke up, the British would come back and gobble up the states one by one, like they done to India. Eamonn believed the Confederacy was nuthin' but the pipe dream of rich men that wouldn't do their own work nor pay anybody to do it."

"Pap told me that some boys in these parts had felt that way. They said it was a rich man's war and poor man's fight. Pap said some had joined the Confederacy, but then deserted and come home. A good many was given refuge around the Sisson's Kingdom area."

"That's right. Some of them boys laid out in caves in the gorges. If they got caught, they was likely to be hung as traitors. But Uncle Eamonn run north to escape.

"When conscriptionists come lookin' for him, the family wouldn't tell where he'd gone. So them rascals set the barn, fields, and lumber mill ablaze. Nothin' was left but char."

"Dang! That was harsh!"

"Right. Some was fixin' to light the house on fire too, but they was shamed out of it. No honor in makin' a woman and babies homeless for the winter."

"What ever become of Eamonn?"

"When West Virginia seceded from the Confederacy and become a state in 1863, he joined the Union army there. He wrote for his regiment's soldier newspaper."

"Did he come home after the war?"

"He wanted to, but feelings was still strong against him. He worked for a newspaper in West Virginia, and earned good money. But he sent most of it back here to his family. After he died, his body was brought back here to rest.

"His mama asked the preacher to say some words at his burial. The preacher told her 'coward' and 'traitor' was the only words he could say about Eamonn Morgan. So Eamonn's mama said if Morgans had to die without the church, we'd live without it, too. Since then, none of us has set foot in any church. We worship in our own house."

"Well, now I understand why you didn't want a church wedding. Mama asked me about that, but I didn't know what to tell her. We got the job done at the courthouse, and that was all I cared about." Virgil put his arm around his wife and pulled her close. "Golly, Katelyn. It's hard to imagine how terrible those war years was for folks 'round here. Neighbors and kin killin' each other. I hope nothin' like that ever happens again in our country."

"Hard times for ever body on both sides," Katelyn agreed. "When I was little, I asked Granny what was a 'oxymoron.' Right away she said, 'civil war.'"

Safina

Katelyn pressed the palms of her hands against her lower back, lifted her chin, and gazed into the sky.

"Let's walk on home now, Virgil."

"Sure. You're probably gettin' hungry, ain't you?"

"A little. And I feel a bit achy."

"Alright. Let's go." Virgil took her hand. They walked toward the tree line that surrounded the cemetery. There, Katelyn stopped.

"Virgil, my water broke," she said calmly.

"Oh, I see. Do you want me to carry you to the house or do you want to walk, honey?"

"I just want to set down here for a spell." Katelyn lowered herself to the ground. She rubbed her belly for a while. Then she placed her hands behind her and stretched. Again, she seemed to be searching the sky. "Isn't this a beautiful place, Virgil? See that cloud up there? How the light behind it is makin' the edges glow brighter than any white in the world."

"Yep. That sure is pretty."

Katelyn took a deep breath. "And you smell that scent of cedar in the air? My sister and I used to play under these trees. See how their tops is swaying so gently in the breeze?" Katelyn brushed her hands over the moss beside her. "This feels softer than any plush blanket. Just listen to the birds singin'. They do sound happy, don't they? Oh, Virgil, honey, I am so happy right now! Beauty and love are all around us. Let's stay in this blessed place. I want everything to happen right here."

Virgil kissed Katelyn's cheek. "Sweetheart, I'm real glad that you feel happy and comfortable. And I know we agreed, but...I was thinkin' it would be indoors—not outside. That's... I don't know, honey. It could be hours."

"I feel it will be soon. Virgil, you know I'm strong and healthy. I've had great care and it's low risk. My doctor's right here with me." She squeezed his hand. "Please, Virgil, trust me. I'm sure I know what to do. Everything I need is right here with me now."

I could not imagine why Katelyn wanted to sit on the ground. Nor did I understand why Virgil wanted her to go to the house. But I was intrigued, so I waited and watched. Virgil sat behind Katelyn and rubbed her back. They talked so quietly to each other, I couldn't hear all that they said.

The bright cloud Katelyn had admired drifted out of sight. Flocks of other clouds migrated from one row of trees to another and disappeared. The sun glided across the sky and shadows shifted.

Katelyn changed her position, too. She stood on hands and knees, rocking forward and back. Then she raised up onto her feet, clutching her bent legs.

Virgil took off his shirt and knelt facing her. Something new was finally happening! Sure they wouldn't notice me, I flew closer.

Virgil put his hands under Katelyn. "Okay. Just push when you feel ready."

I didn't see Katelyn push anything, but she shut her eyes tightly, and voiced a low growl.

Virgil lifted a pink wet thing from the ground beneath her. It hung limply across his hand. He patted it. It made a sound rather like the call of a young fawn that wants its mother. The thing squirmed. It was alive!

Virgil wrapped that living, squalling thing in his shirt. He presented it to Katelyn saying, "You did great, Darlin'. Here's our perfect daughter."

Katelyn folded the daughter thing into her arms and lay back on the moss, smiling with tears on her face.

Virgil kissed his wife's forehead. She stroked the daughter and spoke to it. "Welcome home, sweet Safina. We've been waiting for you." She looked at Virgil and said, "I love you so much. Thank you."

"I love you, Katelyn. Always, with all my heart. Are you ready to go to the house now?"

"Uh-huh."

"Hold on tight to our baby." Virgil lifted Katelyn and carried his family down the path.

I had watched Persons do many very peculiar things, but the events of this day were the most mysterious of all. At last

I understood that the daughter was a baby Person. It's name was Safina. Katelyn was Safina's mama, and Virgil was Safina's daddy. And so I realized at last that Persons do not break into life from shells. They come through broken water.

I.O.U.—Inquire, Observe, Understand

Due to an environmental disaster, most of our flock became refugees. Following a long period of heavy rain, an ice storm and powerful winds had come. All night sharp cracking sounds rang out like gun shots. It was the sound of trees breaking. A gaping wound remained where once our ancient friend had stood and withstood so much. Some of our flock, including Maw and Nate, fled the area. Others nested in surviving trees. But those of us who had lived with Owenasa still long for home.

After the devastating storm had passed and the ground had dried, Virgil and Katelyn climbed the ridge to inspect the damage. When Katelyn saw what had happened to Owenasa, she cried.

Giant machines and a crew of men came to remove fallen trees. They cut Owenasa's enormous body into chunks and hauled them away. Where she had been, new life had already sprouted.

The shed where the Marauder had once been stored had since become a woodworking shop for Virgil. Pieces of Owenasa were delivered there. When he wasn't doctoring, Virgil was often in that shed.

One day I saw Virgil enter the shop. He came out driving a UTV pulling a low trailer. On the trailer was something I recognized. A statue. But this statue wasn't a hunter.

This statue was made of wood. It was the size of a real Person. The Person was a girl. Her head was tilted slightly up. She seemed to be looking ahead toward something higher than herself. One foot was in front of the other. She held a walking stick. A small bird was perched on its end. The girl was wearing overalls and carrying a backpack. Her hair was braided. There was a red pencil in it.

Virgil took out his cell phone. "Honey, come on out here. Bring Granny and Safina. I got a surprise for y'all."

Katelyn came across the yard followed by Granny who was holding Safina's hand. They stopped when they saw the statue. Katelyn stepped forward and touched it. "Oh, Virgil...oh, it's Ashley. How did you...?" She threw her arms around Virgil.

"Happy anniversary, Darlin'. It's that big old pine you loved so much. It's strange, ya' know. When I looked at that trunk, I could sort of visualize this image in it. I just had to carve it out for ya'."

"Virgil, honey, it's a beautiful portrait. A masterpiece! Thank you." Granny gave Virgil a kiss on the cheek.

"I had a lot of help on this piece. It took some special tools and treatments. Some guys with experience carving this kind of old wood coached me by phone and on the internet. Ted is on his way over with some equipment to help me pack it up so it can be stored and moved safely. I wanted y'all to see it first."

Katelyn moved to the statue again and touched some marks at the bottom. "It says, 'I.O.U.—Inquire, Observe, Understand.' You remembered! I told you that was Ashley's motto. Honey, thank you so much! Can we display her in the entrance to the visitor's center?"

Virgil nodded. "I was thinkin' that might be the right place for it."

What, I inquired, was a 'visitors center'?

The Winery

To understand what a 'visitors center' is, I would have to observe. So, I began hanging around the Morgan farm a lot. Then late one morning, when apples were ripe and acorns were brown, I caught a break.

The whole family came out of the house. Katelyn knelt in front of Safina and said, "Give Mama sugar! I'll be right back." The child wrapped her arms around Katelyn's neck and kissed her. "We're meetin' him for lunch at the winery," Katelyn told Granny. "We'll go over plans for the visitors center and for recording the bison release. We won't be long."

"None of y'all drink. Why are ya' goin' to the winery?"

"It was his choice. It's closer to the airport where he's pickin' up Zera this afternoon. Besides, food at the restaurant is great, the weather is perfect, and the view is especially lovely this time of year."

I decided to observe that meeting. On pretty days like this, lots of Persons at the winery sit outside where they have grand views of the surrounding vineyards. I flew straight there and waited on the parking lot.

Virgil's pickup truck pulled in. He and Katelyn took seats at a table with a big umbrella over it. I hid in a nearby hedge.

A shiny silver car parked on the lot. Out stepped a broad-shouldered man with tanned skin, shaggy hair, and a thick red beard. He wore a hat with a narrow, downturned brim. Sunglasses covered his eyes. Colorful tattoos covered his muscular arms from wrists to elbows. Over his T-shirt he wore a khaki vest with many little pockets.

"There he is!" Virgil said. He and Katelyn stood and waved. The man rushed toward them.

They greeted each other with hugs and sat down. Someone came and took their orders. They talked first about their families. I heard the man say, "We're doing great right now! Travel restrictions postponed some of our projects for a while, but we stayed healthy."

"Us, too," said Virgil, "But things were hectic here. We had a lot of cases in this county, and I lost a few patients to the virus. Of course, I didn't want to expose the family, so I slept a lot of nights at the clinic."

"Katelyn, how's your Granny and the baby?"

"Granny's spry as a spring chicken. We've played most venues on The Crooked Road. Safina is talkin' a lot now. Anything she can say in English, she can say in Spanish."

Virgil smiled. "Seems like she carries on conversations with every animal she meets, too."

Katelyn laughed. "We all git so tickled when she tells us what the frog or lamb or duckling are sayin' to her. She's the inspiration for a lot of my children's books."

The man smiled, "That's real cute."

Virgil asked, "How are your folks?"

Before the man could answer, someone brought their meals and beverages. The Persons talked more than they ate. I was hoping to pick up some food scraps after they left.

"They're real good," the man replied. "Right now they're touring Scotland. Daddy said that after seeing me go off to exotic places, they decided to travel while they still had time and health. When Daddy retired as principal, he sold the cattle. They bought a camper and took off to see the USA and Canada. Now they're doing international tours.

"Whenever they come back here, they stay at Elaine's in the apartment Ted built for them over the garage. You know Ted. He built them a really nice place! It even has an elevator, so they won't have to carry things up and down stairs. Daddy signed their house and land over to us. Elaine didn't want her half, so I bought it. I just wanted to keep the house to have a place to stay whenever we come back here."

I knew then that this man was Kevin! He was wearing a disguise, maybe to trick me. Had he come back to catch me again?

"It's so great of you to donate all that acreage to the wildlife restoration project, Kevin! Really generous."

"Glad to do it! What y'all are doing here is so important."

"People have contributed land, funds, and lots of volunteer hours," Katelyn told him. "You know, I used to think my sister wasn't popular. Now I see how much her former classmates and teachers loved and respected her. They've been among the biggest donors—even some who moved out of the area years ago."

"Every adjoining piece of land is precious," Virgil said. "With your donation, the conservation area crosses Charry Ridge and includes a lot more forest, water, and pasture. Papa has worked for years to breed a healthy bison herd that can thrive in these mountains. And by the way, do you remember my cousin Wayne?"

"Sure. The one who enlisted after 9/11. How's he doing these days?"

"He was pretty messed up after his deployments. Papa hired him to work with the bison. Then he helped Wayne get training to become a Conservation Police Officer. He's doing great now. Loves his job. He brings other veterans on tours and shows them what's being accomplished here. He feels the work he does now really is protecting his country."

Kevin smiled, "That's awesome! I'll ask if I can interview him on camera about his experiences with the project."

"Of course, reintroducing native plants and eradicating invasives is a huge part of all this," Katelyn said. "Local veterans' groups, schools, sportsmen, and universities have helped with that. It's really been a community effort."

Kevin was writing on a note pad while they were talking.

"Ted and Elaine have been a wonderful help. Andy's design for the visitors center is a dream come true," Virgil said.

Kevin chuckled. "I think it's Andy's dream come true. He's always said he wanted to design things for his daddy to build. I've seen the plans. Not bad for a budding architect. I want to get footage of the bison release, and we'll do interviews with people who are involved in various ways. We'll return later to film the opening of the visitors center."

"The center will be the perfect place for visitors to get an introduction to the park layout. They'll be able to get familiar with goals of the project, learn about native plants and animals, and hold activities." Virgil said.

So, that's what a visitors center is, I understood!

"Oh, and wait til you see the beautiful portrait of Ashley that Virgil has carved for inside the center!"

"You're still wood carving? Fantastic!" Kevin reached into a pocket in his vest and pulled out a small black object. He set it on the table. "Remember this little crow you made for me when we were kids? It's flown all over the world with me. It's my good luck charm."

Virgil grinned. "No kidding. That's cool!"

"Oh, that reminds me," Katelyn said, reaching into her big purse. "I brought something for you." Katelyn handed Kevin a slender book. "This is my latest. It's a compilation of Ashley's artwork."

Kevin paged through the book, commenting on several drawings. He stopped on one page and jerked back his head. His jaw dropped. "That isn't…me? Is it?"

The Band

"It's you, alright. Ashley showed me that picture right after she drew it."

"How did she…?"

"She said she was walkin' along Charry Ridge when she heard a boy in the woods talkin' to someone. She come up closer, and from behind a tree above you, she saw you talkin' to a crow.

"She said you put a band on its leg and set it free. Then you got on your knees and prayed for God to keep it safe. That's what she drew—you prayin'. She said it made her weep. She told me it was the kindest and bravest thing she'd ever seen a boy do."

Kevin shrugged. "I don't know about that, Katelyn. But it was the only criminal activity I ever engaged in."

Virgil cocked his head. "Criminal? What do you mean? You loved Jet. You took real good care of that bird. I was shocked when you told me you turned it loose."

"Yeah. I didn't know it at the time, of course, but it's illegal to keep a pet crow. It's a violation of the federal Migratory Bird Act.

"Furthermore, you must be over 21 and have a permit to band a wild bird. I just made that band from an aluminum scrap I found in Daddy's workshop. I filed it smooth and shaped it around a drill bit. Later, I fastened it on Jet's leg with a vise grip."

Kevin lowered his head. "I regret what I did to that bird. When I was in the Wildlife Biology program at Lees-McRae, I learned that fledgling crows are often looked after by their parents, even after they've left the nest. Jet might not have been an orphan like I thought.

"And I was never sure if Jet was able to survive in the wild. For all I know, I might actually have fed it to the owls or coyotes.

"That bird meant a lot to me, though. The experience of taking care of Jet and writing that report for school is what fired my interest in birds. I was a better student after that. Ultimately, it led to my career as a videographer and gave me the opportunity to travel the world filming wildlife and making documentaries about conservation efforts. I just wish I'd known then what I know now."

Katelyn patted Kevin's hand. Virgil said, "Don't be hard on yourself, buddy. We were just kids. Your intentions were all good."

Kevin stood up and said, "Yeah…Well, my friends, I'd better get rollin'. Got to pick up Zera. She's flying her own plane in to the county airport." He picked up the checks and said, "This is on me."

"Thanks, Kevin. Granny's expecting y'all over for breakfast." Katelyn said.

"We're looking forward to it. Can't wait to see her and Safina." Kevin held up the book. "Thanks again! I'll treasure this, Katelyn." Kevin paid and strolled back toward his car.

I got there before he did and waited. Kevin had changed and I hadn't recognized him. I wondered if he would recognize me now. So I hid my right foot under my belly feathers.

Kevin noticed me as he approached. He slowed his pace. He grinned and spoke softly. "Hey there. You make a splendid hood ornament, but I'm gonna need to move that vehicle pretty soon."

He looked me over and saw that I was balancing on one foot. His brow creased. "Uh-oh. What's happened? Did you catch that awful staph infection that makes a crow's foot fall off?"

I lowered my foot. He saw the band and gasped. "Jet? Can it… Is it really you? After all these years!" He closed his eyes and muttered something. Was he talking to Heavenly Father or to himself? No way to tell.

When he opened his eyes, his mustache stretched wide across his face, and he smiled with all his teeth. "I'm soooo glad to see you!" He didn't try to touch me, but he offered his left arm to see if I would perch there. I wasn't afraid of him any more, so I did. A ring on his finger glinted in the sunlight. I pecked it.

He chuckled. "Yeah. I got banded, too. Her name is Zera. You'd like each other."

I bobbed my head approvingly. I spread my wings, flapped a couple of times, and rose into the air.

Before I flew away, I said, "Bye-bye."

Acknowledgments

I thank my dear friends, Pamela and Dan Murphy, for their feedback on early drafts, and for Pamela's drawing which contributes so meaningfully to the cover design.

For sharing information about the publishing process, I am grateful to Dan Olson, and to Jack Wright and Sharon Hatfield. For help with choosing wording that is authentic to the region, I thank my sweet neighbors, Betty and C. T. Gardner.

Much appreciation goes to Alice Bingner, my long-time friend and mentor.

Great thanks to Kate Long for permission to include lyrics from her splendid original song "Who Will Watch the Home Place."

Thanks also to Bryan Bowers for allowing me to post his recording of the traditional folksong "The Blackest Crow" on my author website.

From the time this little story began pecking around in my head, trying to hatch, Tim Smith encouraged me to nurture it and helped me to set it free. I am forever grateful for his support and for his skill in formatting, editing, and publishing this book. He is my partner in all things and the wind beneath my wings.

About the Author

A native of eastern Ohio, Suzann Albright graduated from Miami University. During the 1980's, she taught middle- and high school-age students in rural West Virginia where she met and married her late husband. After graduate school, she provided early intervention technical assistance and developed professional training materials at the University of South Carolina Center for Disability Resources.

She has a deep appreciation for the landscape, history and the rich culture of Appalachia—a region often misunderstood or underrepresented in popular literature.

Now retired, Suzann lives on several acres near the Blue Ridge Parkway with her partner Tim and their English Labrador Retriever. She raises gardens, reads, and takes lots of online courses. She's intrigued by the various wild animals near her home, and hopes they enjoy wondering about her, too.

Crossing Charry Ridge is Suzann's first novel.

About the Illustrator

Pamela Murphy grew up in Florida, graduated from Erskine College, and received a Masters Degree from the University of South Carolina. She and her husband Dan lived in West Virginia where the Appalachian landscape and animals became the focus of her drawings and block prints.

They moved to St. Helena Island, South Carolina in the 1980's, where they raised their children Miranda and Dylan, and Pamela taught art in high schools.

After retirement, Pamela and Dan lived in the Florida Keys and Mexico. They currently live on Little Torch Key, Florida. Pamela enjoys spending time with Dan and their children and pets, volunteering for state parks, ecology group beach and mangrove cleanups, and traveling. She works on marine life paintings, art projects, and learning languages.